CHEVROLET SATURDAYS

CHEVROLET SATURDAYS

Candy Dawson Boyd

Macmillan Publishing Company New York

Maxwell Macmillan Canada Toronto

Maxwell Macmillan International

New York Oxford Singapore Sydney

Macmillan Publishing Company is part of the Maxwell Communication Group of Companies. Macmillan Publishing Company, 866 Third Avenue, New York, NY 10022. Maxwell Macmillan Canada, Inc., 1200 Eglinton Avenue East, Suite 200, Don Mills, Ontario M3C 3N1.

First edition
Printed in the United States of America

1 3 5 7 9 10 8 6 4 2

The text of this book is set in 11 point ITC Garamond Light.

Library of Congress Cataloging-in-Publication Data
Boyd, Candy Dawson.
Chevrolet Saturdays / Candy Dawson Boyd. — 1st ed.
p. cm.
Summary: When he enters fifth grade after his mother's remarriage, Joey has trouble adjusting to his new teacher and to his new stepfather.
ISBN 0-02-711765-0
[1. Remarriage—Fiction. 2. Stepfathers—Fiction. 3. Schools—Fiction. 4. Afro Americans—Fiction.] I. Title.
PZ7.B69157Chf 1993 [Fic]—dc20 92-32119

To my father and mother,
who gave me knowledge of my heritage,
determination, and confidence

1

The alarm sounded like the shriek of an ambulance. Joey buried his head, but the noise persisted. Surrendering, he threw back the comforter and stumbled across the bedroom floor. He slammed the button down. Outside the door he heard his mother's voice and the low rumble of Mr. Johnson's response.

Joey sighed as he regarded the photograph hung on the wall over the alarm clock. There stood his family. "My own family," he whispered, rubbing the sleep out of his eyes. The photograph was of his father, his mother, and him standing by the Christmas tree two years before. Not long after that, his father had moved out. Then, following a wedding during the previous April, Mr. Johnson had moved in. Joey still couldn't accept that his mother was married to another man.

Feeling the familiar knot in his stomach, Joey turned away from the photograph. Before him stretched another endless school day with Mrs. Hamlin, his fifth-grade teacher. An unopened math book lay on the desk across from his bed. He glanced at it. Then he made his way to the bathroom, oblivious to the bright Berkeley October sunshine.

Forty minutes later, Joey had dressed, gulped down a bowl of cold cereal, and ducked past his mother. He was three blocks away when he remembered that he had left his math book in his bedroom. Shrugging his shoulders, he pedaled toward school.

Even before Joey saw Mrs. Hamlin standing by the classroom door, her thin lips pressed together, he knew this was going to be a bad Thursday. He headed for his seat.

No matter how hard he tried, he couldn't forget what had happened as he was leaving home. He had raced through the kitchen, stepping over Mr. Johnson's Airedale terrier, Josie, and ignoring his mother as she reminded him to make sure he was ready for school. Then, just as he'd hopped onto his bike, Mr. Johnson had appeared at the front door and waved to him. Joey had managed to mumble, "Good morning, Mr. Johnson." But as he was escaping, his mother had come to stand beside her new husband. In his mind Joey had seen her gaze down the steps at him with sad, dark eyes.

Joey lowered his head onto the desk. Why can't Mama understand how I feel? Mr. Johnson isn't my daddy or uncle or even my friend, like Doc. He's still a stranger to me, a man who lives in our house. Not a bad man or even a mean one. But I want my daddy back home.

"What's the problem today?" asked Denise, her eyes wide and alert.

Joey looked up at her. "I left my math book at home. Plus I didn't do my homework."

Denise shook her head. "Not again."

"This is getting to be a habit with you," added D.J., plopping his book bag down onto his desk.

"You want to copy my homework?" offered Denise. She tossed her thick braids and smiled at him through metal braces.

"No, thanks," Joey said, shoving D.J.'s jab aside. His best friend, D.J. Tyler, sat in the same cluster. But so did Denise Hopkins, and no matter what he did, she would not leave him alone.

"Joey's got a girlfriend," teased D.J. "Joey's got a girlfriend."

"You got eyelashes like a girl!" said Joey, hitting D.J. where it hurt the most. D.J., short for Donald James, was the youngest of six children. The other five were girls: Lena, Sherelle, Monique, Gloria, and Tiffany the Terror. D.J. had the longest eyelashes in the entire family, a fact that he detested.

"So what? You're the one without your math homework. You're the one Mrs. Hamlin is going to get!" said D.J.

"Yeah, and you got the brains of a starfish," said Joey. He watched D.J. mull that one over. Even though D.J. went to gifted class, Joey could stump him with science. At least I'm gifted there, thought Joey.

"Okay," D.J. said, "I give up. What does that mean?"

"Starfish don't have any brains." Joey laughed.

"No brains?" Denise asked.

"Not a one," Joey said.

Suddenly Mrs. Hamlin was right beside him. "Well, you have a brain, even though you don't use it much. Let's see how well it worked last night." Mrs. Hamlin ignored the snickers around her. "Joey, I want to see your math homework."

Aware of the kids staring at him, Joey reached for his book bag and rummaged through the papers and books. Finally, he threw his hands up in the air.

"I must have left it at home."

"Just like last week and the week before," Mrs. Hamlin said. "You've got to start getting serious about school, Joey. I mean it. Half the time I think that you don't care about anything."

The school buzzer sounded. Someone pulled the classroom door shut. Kids were milling around, talking and playing. The noise level increased. Abruptly, Mrs. Hamlin turned and hurried to the front of the room. "I want this room quiet by the time I count to ten!"

Joey watched to see what would happen. It was the same every morning, but there was always hope.

"One. Two. Three. Four. Five." Her voice could barely be heard above the laughter and chatter.

"Six. Seven. Eight."

Most kids had taken their seats, but the hard core remained standing together, just as they did every morning. Clark Miller and Anthony Carpenter were the worst of them.

Mrs. Hamlin began to move toward the group, still counting. "Nine. Nine and a half." She paused.

As the group headed slowly for their seats, Joey shook his head. Most of class time was spent dealing with that bunch.

At last Mrs. Hamlin completed the count. "Ten!" At that instant, the group slumped into their seats, grinning at one another. Except for Clark Miller. He had ambled over to the pencil sharpener.

"Clark, take your seat! Now!" Mrs. Hamlin's voice screeched like a piece of chalk dragged across the blackboard.

Slowly, Clark took his pencil out of the sharpener, examined the tip, stuffed it into his pocket, and eventually reached his seat across from Joey. Then, still standing, he swept the room with his light-blue eyes. He looked like a king surveying his subjects.

"Class, take out your math homework. Place it on the outer corner of your desks to be collected. Get out your math list for this week. Write each word twenty-five times," the teacher ordered. "Denise, collect the homework."

Groans and protests filled the room.

"I don't want to hear a sound! Not a sound! Or your name goes up on the board!"

Joey searched for his list as Mrs. Hamlin snatched a piece of chalk and wrote a name on the board. Clark was reading a football magazine.

"Clark Miller! No recess!"

"But I wasn't doing anything!" He jumped up and balled his hands into fists.

"Sit back down before I call the office and have them send for your father." Mrs. Hamlin's thin face puffed out with anger.

The class waited as Clark eased back into his seat and stuffed the magazine into his desk. He took out his list.

Joey began writing *equation* twenty-five times. His mind drifted. He stopped to stare out the window.

Mornings had been so different in Miss Alder's room. Last year, even with his parents' divorce, life had been better because of his fourth-grade teacher. But she really liked me, Joey thought. And she was a good teacher, not like Mrs. Hamlin. He eyed his classmates.

Everybody knew that new teachers got more than their share of difficult kids, but Miss Alder had been new, too. Joey wished he were back on the storytelling rug, listening to the clear, quiet sound of her voice. In his mind he could see his name on the bulletin board, just above Miss Alder's head: Joey Davis, Science Center Leader.

Miss Alder had even recommended that he be tested for gifted class. She always told me I was smart, he thought.

Smart, like D.J. and Denise. Joey smiled, feeling warm inside.

"Joey! Why aren't you working? Anthony, how can you write without a pencil or pen?" Mrs. Hamlin stalked the room.

Joey shoved those memories to the side and concentrated on the work before him.

"That's better. Class, stand for the Pledge of Allegiance."

The morning proceeded at its normal erratic pace. When recess ended, Joey meandered toward his cluster. He couldn't bury the thought of his mother and Mr. Johnson in the morning sunlight. For some reason, the sight of the two of them framed together in the front door stuck in his memory.

Suddenly, Joey tripped over a foot. He fell, grasping for a desk or chair. But there was none. When he struggled up, pain shot through his left ankle.

"Who tripped me?" Joey yelled, searching the faces around him. No one answered. Clark Miller's blue eyes revealed nothing. Joey knew that Clark was behind most of the trouble in the room. Anthony Carpenter, a bully who was one assault away from expulsion, smirked. Anthony operated as Clark's backup.

"What's going on here?" Mrs. Hamlin pushed her way through the crowd of children.

"Somebody tripped me!" Joey glared at the two boys, convinced that it had been one of them.

"Who saw Joey fall?" asked Mrs. Hamlin, running her hand through tangled hair.

Joey waited. Clark and Anthony created mischief just to have something to do. But he wasn't going to let either of them think that they could pick on him. Once they started, nothing could stop them. He had seen this happen with other boys who were too afraid to fight back.

Joey faced them. "I know that one of you tripped me! You try anything again and you'll be sorry!" he shouted. "You hear me, Clark and Anthony? I'm not scared of you two. Leave me alone or you'll both be on the floor!" Turning away, Joey limped to his seat.

"And I'm not going to have threats in my classroom. Joey, you go to the nurse. Then sit in the office until you cool off. Denise, go with him. Alexander, turn off the lights. I want you all in your seats with heads down by the count of ten! One . . ."

Joey hobbled toward the door. Knowing that his classmates were watching, he exaggerated the limp, even though the pain wasn't that bad. Denise ran to open the door. When she reached to take his arm, he resisted.

The hall was empty. As they were passing the door to room 207, it opened. A slender, red-headed woman stepped out, her hands full of papers, a stapler, and letters cut out of construction paper. The pile shifted, and multicolored alphabet letters scattered like crisp autumn leaves around her feet.

"I'll get them for you, Miss Alder." Joey rushed over.

"Hey! What about your ankle?" asked Denise.

"Joey and Denise, it's good to see you. As usual, I'm trying to do six things at once. Thanks. I want to get these essays up before lunch," said Miss Alder. "How are you doing?"

"We both want you to be our teacher," said Denise, handing the woman a handful of letters. "Joey got sent to the office and he didn't do anything! Our teacher doesn't like him or any of us. All she does is holler and yell. I don't think she likes kids much."

"Now, Denise, things can't be that bad. Joey, what's going on?"

"I wish I was back in your room. I'd give anything if you could be my teacher. I hate being in Mrs. Hamlin's room!" he blurted out.

"Oh, Joey." Miss Alder put her pile on the floor and moved closer to Joey. He smelled her lemon-scented cologne. "Give Mrs. Hamlin a chance. You know that this is her first year."

"Last year was your first year, and you were the best teacher I've ever had," said Joey.

"The best!" Denise chimed in.

"Be patient, Joey. And keep a low profile." Miss Alder peered into her classroom. Joey knew that her kids were busy working. "I'll talk to her about you. After all, you were my science-center leader. How's the science going?"

"She doesn't like science, so we only read the book and answer questions," Denise murmured.

"Oh." For a long moment, Miss Alder was quiet. "You two better get on. Wait a sec. What do you wish, Joey?"

He smiled. That had been their favorite game. Whenever he'd come to school feeling depressed about the divorce, Miss Alder had asked him to make a wish that included a science fact. The wish had to relate to something that had happened to him.

Joey thought for a moment. "I wish I was a great white shark, thirty feet long, with thousands of teeth. Actually, it's light gray, not white."

Shaking her head, Miss Alder chuckled. "Okay, why, Joey?"

"Because the great white shark is the only creature in the sea who has no natural enemies. Even killer whales leave it alone. And if I was a great white shark, no one would ever bother me. Not even Mrs. Hamlin."

"Not even Mrs. Hamlin," Denise echoed.

"Congratulations! You get top points for that one. Now get going and remember what I said."

Joey moved away with Denise. He didn't want her to overhear what he had to ask Miss Alder.

"Miss Alder, did you talk with Mrs. Hamlin about getting me tested for you-know-what?" he whispered.

"Yes, I certainly did. I told her what to do." She crossed her fingers. "Give her some time."

Feeling hopeful, Joey let Denise help him get settled in the nurse's small cubicle. The nurse examined Joey's ankle. There was only minor swelling, but she wrapped it anyway. Then Joey and Denise went to the office. Joey took a seat on the bench. Denise left. Fifteen minutes later, Mrs. Hamlin called the office and asked that Joey be sent back to the room.

For the rest of the day, other than handing him a note to take home, Mrs. Hamlin ignored Joey. Clark glowered at him, since Mrs. Hamlin gave Clark a note as well. Joey focused on his reading work sheets. Then he borrowed D.J.'s math book and finished the homework from the previous night.

When D.J. and Denise lined up for gifted class with five other students, Joey cringed inside. He knew there was a special test he could take to see if he was smart enough to be in gifted, but he had to be referred by his parents and his teacher or principal and pass the test—or get real high scores for any two years on the annual statewide examination.

Joey knew he had just missed the high-score cutoff for years. Fighting parents, separation, and then the divorce had taken their toll. Sometimes I didn't even try. I just picked any answer, he thought.

In any event, the gifted program's budget had been cut. There had been no room for more students. So Miss Alder's referral and that of his parents had gotten him nowhere last year.

But D.J. said that three kids have left the gifted class, so there's space for me now if I can get referred and pass that test, thought Joey. There's no way Mrs. Hamlin will refer me. She thinks I'm lazy and dumb.

D.J. and the rest of the "brains" returned to the room as the school day ended. Several of the children didn't wait for Mrs. Hamlin to dismiss them. They poured out of the room. Joey remained at his desk, determined to follow Miss Alder's advice.

"Well, at least some children in this room know how to behave. I am pleasantly surprised. Line up and walk out," she said. "And, Joey, don't forget to bring that note back, signed. I want your parents to know that your lack of concentration is a serious problem."

On the way out, Joey glanced back. Mrs. Hamlin stood in the doorway. Tall and big-boned, she had tufts of dark hair that stuck out in every direction. She raised her hand to her forehead as if to ward off an attack. Without warning, she slumped against the door frame. For some reason, Joey felt sorry for her.

"Hey, come on, Joey," yelled D.J., taking the stairs two at a time. Denise trailed behind.

Outside the boys jumped onto their bicycles, while Denise caught the yellow school bus. As Joey skirted the street traffic, he let out a loud whoop. Bay winds swirled around him. He breathed in the smells of the trees.

Pedaling faster, Joey passed D.J. As the wheels spun, Joey's spirits lightened. Mrs. Hamlin, Clark and Anthony, his wrapped ankle, gifted class, even the note in his book bag, faded from his mind. He turned the corner and stopped in front of Doc's drugstore. D.J. braked next to him. The boys locked their bikes and entered the old building.

Joey's eyes adjusted to the change in light. Tiny red and green Christmas tree lights lined the woodwork along the ceiling of the drugstore and winked on and off. Doc kept them lit all year. He always said, "You never know when you're going to need Christmas."

The festive lights stirred up memories of past holidays. Mama singing carols while they decorated the tree. And Daddy. Daddy coming in with huge, mysterious boxes. Daddy driving him to the Nature Company, where together they examined and enjoyed the colorful animal books, posters, maps, and models. Daddy slicing the Thanksgiving turkey. Daddy wheeling out his new bike at Christmas two years ago. Daddy.

Who will I be with this Thanksgiving and Christmas? Mama and Mr. Johnson? Or Daddy? The ebullient feeling inside his chest evaporated. Right now Joey didn't need to think about patched-together holidays. What he needed was to see Doc.

2

Above the sounds of customers' voices, Joey heard many of the three dozen or so wall clocks chime, tick, bong, and cuckoo, cuckoo, cuckoo. It was almost four o'clock. Joey smiled, knowing how much Doc delighted in his collection and in saying to anyone who dared to complain, "Time is precious. Not the right time, but *time.* And the only *right* time is now."

To Joey's right stood the original 1940 soda fountain. His eyes scanned the three aisles crowded with unpacked goods.

In the rear of the drugstore was the pharmacy. It had been closed for three years. Joey moved over to the second aisle. D.J. followed. There was Doc, a short, white-haired man, bent over as he stocked the shelf with cough syrup. With a loud groan, he stood up, massaging his lower back.

"Finally, fortune shines upon me. Joey, hey, man, rescue me and finish stocking these shelves while I take care of my customers," Doc said, patting Joey's shoulder. "Save my back."

"Hi, Doc. Sure. Can D.J. help, too?"

"You bet!" Doc laughed. "I need all the assistance I can get."

For the next twenty minutes, the boys unloaded merchandise and stocked the shelves. Above them, music from Doc's elaborate stereo system played through speakers placed in each corner of the store. The magic of Oscar Peterson, Sarah Vaughan, Shirley Horn, John Coltrane, Betty Carter, Wynton Marsalis, and other jazz stars soared and swooped up and down the aisles.

Eventually the boys emptied the cartons. Aware that Doc liked his store shiny and neat, Joey and D.J. carried the boxes to the storeroom.

Six red stools lined the front of the old-fashioned soda fountain. The boys chose the middle two. Chrome gleamed. Even the wooden picture frames shone. On every available wall space hung photographs of Doc fishing and of his wife Elizabeth and their five children and nine grandchildren. There were photographs of numerous graduations, including seven from various colleges. Doc had placed blue ribbons on those. The full names of all of his children were displayed in bold print.

Joey spotted his favorite photograph, of his father, his mother, Doc and his family, and Joey at a church anniversary picnic. There on that wall was the family he wanted back so desperately. The family that had been snatched away from him. They didn't ask me what to do, he thought. I didn't get a say about Daddy's leaving. It's not fair! They divorce, and I have to live with it whether I agree or not. He propped his head in his left hand.

"What's that woebegone expression on your face, my friend?" asked Doc.

Joey wiped at the unexpected tears. Silently, D.J. handed him a napkin.

"Well, I guess this means that I am required to produce one of my magical concoctions, a miracle guaranteed to erase sadness and replace it with gladness," said Doc. "This definitely calls for a Feel Better Cause You Can't Fall Apart triple chocolate soda à la Doc Matthews. How about one, D.J.?"

"Oh, yes, sir!" D.J. beamed his appreciation. He nudged Joey.

"Thanks, Doc. I need a Feel Better soda." Joey placed the wadded napkin on the counter.

"How is life at that institution of higher learning that you two attend?" asked Doc, piling chocolate ice cream into two fancy glasses.

"Horrible," said Joey.

D.J. nodded in agreement.

"It's not that way for you, D.J. Mrs. Hamlin doesn't bother you. She likes all the kids who go to gifted," protested Joey. "That zaps me."

"Mrs. Hamlin is having trouble handling the class," D.J. explained. "Sometimes things are a disaster. Joey seems to attract her attention at the worst times." D.J. twisted on the stool. "I don't know why she leaves me alone. I just stay quiet."

Doc nodded at D.J. "Joey, how is life at home?"

A thick silence covered the counter. Joey soaked in the sounds and sights around him. Christmas lights that never went out, clocks that kept their own time, photographs capturing past moments from the lives of people he loved. And Doc with his Feel Better sodas.

Joey stared at the church picnic photograph taken three years ago, not too long before Doc's wife died of cancer. Daddy had just told a joke. Joey hadn't understood the punch line, but he'd laughed, anyway. Everyone in the snapshot, especially Daddy and Mama, seemed so happy, as if they would feel that same way forever.

Joey watched Doc pour Hershey's chocolate and seltzer water from a black hose over the ice cream. Joey shrugged. "Mama spends most of her time with Mr. Johnson. I miss Daddy so much. Mama gets mad at me and unhappy because I call him Mr. Johnson."

Doc dropped chocolate sprinkles, chocolate-covered raisins, and walnuts over the sodas. He topped them with whipped cream and two cherries. "Home appears to be as unpredictable and joyous a place for you as your classroom," he commented. "Sometimes we are so blessed, and you are truly one of the most fortunate of young men, Joey, my boy."

With a flourish, Doc placed the sodas in front of the boys, grabbing a cherry from each and popping them into his mouth. The whipped cream glistened like frosting on his mustache. Doc dipped his spoon into Joey's soda, and chocolate ice cream dribbled down his chin. He wiped his mouth. "What a spectacular soda!"

Joey couldn't help but grin. No matter what, Doc managed to cheer him up. D.J. smiled, too. The boys dug their spoons into the delicious ice cream, while Doc left to wait on a customer.

Soon he returned. "So, Joey, my boy, I know that you are wondering what makes you the most fortunate of young men." Doc's brown eyes twinkled behind his glasses. "Because you are alive, my boy, alive and confronted with all of the challenges that accompany this strange state of being."

"Sometimes I'd rather be dead," Joey muttered.

Doc pounded the counter with his hand. The salt and pepper shakers danced. "Don't you ever say that!" His voice boomed above the husky strains of Sarah Vaughan singing "Black Coffee."

Joey and D.J. jumped.

"Life is no joke. I was there when you were born. I knew your mother when she was a little girl. Your parents love you. Just because they decided to divorce doesn't mean they divorced you. Life is a gift. And I don't want to ever hear you saying that you don't want it. You hear me!" The creases on Doc's dark brown face deepened. Joey could count the times he had seen Doc get angry.

"I'm sorry, Doc. I didn't mean it," Joey said, his appetite gone. "I want Daddy and Mama to be together. I wish we were a real family. Not all split up. They didn't ask me what I thought about them breaking up. Didn't they know they broke me up, too?" Joey held back the tears; he wasn't a crybaby.

D.J. continued to consume his soda, his eyes fixed on Doc.

Doc took a deep breath and let it out. "I want my family back the way it was before, too. Before my wife, Elizabeth, passed away. I want to stand back there in the pharmacy and be able to see her at the counter or the cash register. But no matter what I wish, the harsh fact is that Elizabeth is gone. Life changes, Joey. And the ones who prevail do the best they can." Doc turned away and rewound one of the clocks on the wall.

"How do you prevail, Doc?" asked D.J.

Joey listened intently, pushing his soda aside.

"I work. I work hard, here at the drugstore, in my church, and helping my family. Work gives me a great deal of solace and joy," he said, touching a photograph of his wife.

The soda forgotten, Joey nodded when D.J. indicated that he wanted to finish it. "I want Daddy and Mama back together. Mr. Johnson can leave and marry somebody else," said Joey.

"No way," said D.J., his mouth smeared with chocolate ice cream. "He's not leaving your mama. No way, Joey."

"I wouldn't put my money on that man leaving you and

your mother. You'd better think again. Well, my boy, you've got plenty of hard work to do. Nobody can deal with these problems for you. But you are always welcome here for a Feel Better soda," offered Doc.

"I don't know what to do, Doc," said Joey.

"You'll figure it out. You're an African-American boy, growing into manhood. This is one of your first real tests."

"What do you mean?" asked Joey.

"Well, you may get the opportunity to make your way to one of several doors. If you select the right door and make it through, you walk taller, hold your head higher, and move closer to becoming a solid man. But getting to the right door can be painful and lonely." Doc stopped.

"And what happens if you don't choose the right door, Doc?" D.J. leaned forward, his soda forgotten. Joey frowned.

"Then you stumble. And if you make too many wrong choices, you fall so far, so fast, that you lose your chance to become a solid African-American man who walks this world with his head on straight. You become what I call a shadow man. A terrible, tragic loss. Hey, I got a store to run." Doc walked off.

"Doc talks in riddles," Joey said to D.J.

D.J. agreed.

Not long after, Joey put his hand out to Doc to say good-bye. Doc hugged both boys to him and gave them a push out the door.

At a corner two streets over, Joey and D.J. parted. Joey pedaled slowly. Reaching home, he stopped. A woman was entering his mother's beauty shop, Ernestine's Palace of Beauty. He heard laughter and talk. Josie, the Airedale terrier, barked and dashed about behind the locked gate.

Following the late-afternoon routine, Joey wheeled his bike to the new gate by the side of the house. He took out the key Mr. Johnson had given him and opened the gate, careful not to let Josie get out. Josie sniffed at his heels as he leaned his bike against the side of the garage, checked her water bowl, and let himself into the kitchen, opening another locked door. He heard Josie whimpering, but he didn't let her in. Except when it rained, Mr. Johnson liked his dog to be in the yard during the day.

After grabbing a handful of oatmeal-raisin cookies, Joey went out the back door and entered the beauty shop from the rear, through the small storeroom. Mama was busy shampooing a customer's hair. He called hello to the two beauticians who rented chairs from her, Gladys and Susie. Georgia was up front, filing nails.

"Hi. How did school go today?" asked his mother.

Joey liked the way she looked, pretty and compact. Her ebony eyes rested on him like warm hands. Then he remembered the note in his pants pocket. "Not so great. Mrs. Hamlin got mad because I didn't have my math homework. But I finished it in school and turned it in. She gave me a note for you to read and sign," said Joey in a hushed tone, pulling out the piece of paper.

His mother applied conditioner to her customer's hair and wiped her hands on a towel. She read the note. "She says you show little or no interest in school."

"I know. I read it. But it's not true. I try the best I can," said Joey, not caring who heard.

"Oh, Joey, if it's not one problem, it's another. You never got bad notes before. I don't understand you anymore. Hand me that pen. Then take the garbage out back. Set the table for dinner and do your homework." Without another word, she signed the note, gave it to him, and returned to work. Joey's shoulders drooped.

As he was laying out three dinner plates, the telephone rang. Joey reached it before the third ring, a game he liked to play.

"Joey, it's Daddy. How's my man doing?" His father's excited voice echoed across the telephone lines.

"Daddy! Are you coming by to get me now, instead of tomorrow night? Can we go to the zoo on Saturday? Can I spend Saturday night with you?" Joey's heart raced.

"Hold on, son. I'm on my way to Chicago. I called to tell you that I won't be able to pick you up tomorrow," his father said. "But I'll make it up to you as soon as I return. We'll do anything you want. I promise."

Joey's spirits sank. This was not the first time his father had called to cancel their plans, but why was he going to Chicago?

Joey slumped into the kitchen chair by the phone. "I want to see you, Daddy. Will you be back on Sunday?"

"I don't think so. Things are moving fast, Joey. I've got a shot at the job I've worked for, for years. Not just handling automobile claims, but something bigger. This is the chance of a lifetime for me. You understand that, don't you?" his father asked.

"No, Daddy. Why are you flying to Chicago? When are you coming home? When will I see you?"

"As soon as I get back. Look, Joey, nothing is signed and dated yet, so I don't want to say anything definite until I'm sure. Son, I've got to run. Airplanes don't wait. Talk to you soon. Tell your mama hello from me. Be a good boy." The line went dead. Joey heard footsteps behind him.

"I came to check on your progress. Mrs. Taylor is under the dryer, so I get a break," said his mother, rifling through the stack of mail on the kitchen table.

When Joey didn't respond, she looked up.

"What's the matter?" His mother waited. Then she flung the mail down on the table. "Your father called, didn't he? And he told you that he wouldn't be picking you up this weekend because he's got some big, important deal going. Right? No, don't even bother to answer, don't even bother. Was he at home or work?" She grabbed the receiver.

"Mama, Daddy's leaving on an airplane, to Chicago."

"Chicago! What is he going to do there?" She slammed the phone down.

"He said something about the chance of a lifetime and nothing being signed yet. Mama, is Daddy moving to Chicago?" Joey asked.

"Who knows what that man is planning." Then her voice softened. She knelt down. "Look, honey, your daddy is trying to get his life together. I don't mean to speak harshly of him, but I can't stand it when he disappoints you. Come on. Perhaps this time he's going to get a real break. I hope so. You want to bring your homework down to the shop?"

All Joey wanted was to be alone. "No, thanks, Mama." She embraced him.

Joey was folding the last napkin when the telephone rang again. He rushed to get it. Maybe it was Daddy calling to say that his plans had changed and that he would be by on

Friday after all. But it was a strange man asking to talk with Mr. Franklin Johnson.

At that moment, the front door opened. Joey's stepfather walked in.

"Mr. Johnson, some man wants to speak to you." Joey handed over the telephone and started upstairs.

"Just a minute," his stepfather said to the man on the telephone. His bass voice rumbled out the words. "Joey, do me a favor and get me some paper and a pencil."

Joey obeyed, barely meeting his stepfather's eyes. Outside Josie was yelping her head off. A gesture from Mr. Johnson let Joey know that he could let her in.

From the kitchen, even above Josie's grateful yelps, he heard a kind of enthusiasm in his stepfather's voice that he had not heard before.

"It runs? Great! Great! And it's a '53 Chevy? Just what I need!" Mr. Johnson grinned at Joey. "How about tonight? Give me directions. Let's talk money after I see it. A couple of hours at the most. Thanks for calling, Mr. Rathmussen. I'm on my way!"

Josie scampered over and leaped at Mr. Johnson. He rubbed her head.

"Joey, I've got to leave. Seems like that ad I placed for a 1953 Chevrolet pickup truck is going to pay off. Want to come with me?" Mr. Johnson's face glowed.

"Thanks, Mr. Johnson, but Mama told me to do my homework."

Some of the joy drained away from Mr. Johnson's expression. "I see. Feed Josie for me. I'll tell your mama where I'm going on my way out." As he turned to leave, he stopped.

"Joey, is something bothering you? You don't look quite right."

Joey shook his head. He had to be careful. He sensed that Mr. Johnson watched him even when he didn't realize it.

Later that evening, after a dinner of Crockpot stew, Joey roused himself from his math book as the front door opened. Curious, he left his bedroom and sat on the top step. He overheard Mr. Johnson telling his mother about the '53 Chevy truck. His mother giggled.

"Joey, I'm driving Franklin out to Martinez. Come on with us."

"No, thanks, Mama. I've got more homework to do. I'll be fine here with Josie."

When the front door closed, Joey flopped onto his bed. Josie was stretched out downstairs by the front door. She seemed to spend most of her life waiting for Mr. Johnson to come home. Just like I spend my time waiting for Daddy to call and come and get me, Joey thought.

Joey stared out the window of his room. It overlooked the backyard. Redwood planter boxes full of withered pansies and petunias encircled the small concrete patio. Warm weather had retreated too soon. Cool days and chilly nights signaled an early, wet winter.

Mr. Johnson's labor on the garage was evident. New doors and bars on the windows as well as coats of blue paint covered years of neglect. Tired, Joey decided to take a nap. Dog, his old stuffed toy, lay in a corner of the bed.

A heavy grinding sound jolted him awake. Josie howled. To his surprise, Joey saw a huge, old pickup truck lumber into the backyard. With a series of shudders and thumps, the truck stopped. He watched his stepfather jump out and open the garage. Then he closed it. The truck seemed too large to fit into any garage in the neighborhood. Besides, their garage was crammed with tools and equipment. For a moment, Mr. Johnson stared at the sky. Then, to Joey's amazement, he leaped into the evening air.

"Joey! Get downstairs. We're having a party! Hurry up!" called his mother.

Joey squinted at the strange truck and then sprinted downstairs. Mama was taking out cartons of ice cream and dishes. Mr. Johnson came in, kissed her, and they sashayed around the kitchen, singing. Josie jumped about. Joey stood still.

"Joey! Did you see the new truck? Isn't it something else? Come on out and take a look. My dream truck. Now I can really get my contracting business started. Right, pretty mama?" Mr. Johnson kissed his mother. Joey flinched.

"Right on, Mr. Contractor," said his mother, including Joey in her smile.

They went out into the backyard. The pickup truck was much larger than Joey had thought it was. Chipped and scarred, it needed paint. On the side Joey saw wide running boards. He stepped up onto one and peeked in. It was dark inside. He walked around the 1953 Chevrolet pickup truck. The front rose like the prow of an ancient ship.

"Joey, you are looking at one of the best pickup trucks ever built, a three-quarter–ton beauty." Mr. Johnson slapped the hood with pride. "Needs some tires, springs, and shocks, but it's in great shape."

"Needs to be painted," mumbled Joey, who was dwarfed by the truck.

"Well, what do you think? Wait until we go for a ride in this baby! You've never experienced anything like it. Makes you feel like the king of the road. Installing security systems for Hudson Corporation is going to be easier, knowing that at last I have this fine vehicle." Mr. Johnson ran his hand over the grill.

"I never saw a truck like this one. Did it cost a lot of money?" Joey stood by the side. Somehow talking to Mr. Johnson about the truck wasn't hard.

"Not as much as I thought. I wish you had come with me. This guy, Rathmussen, in Martinez, bought it a few years ago from a man who had farmed with it for over twenty years. Rathmussen lost interest in it. Imagine wanting to get rid of this." Mr. Johnson ran his hands along the rusted side of the door. "Joey, wait until I fix this truck up. Even the chrome will shine."

Joey did some figuring in his head. "Your truck—"

Mr. Johnson held up his hand. "Wait a minute there. This isn't any *your* truck deal, Joey. This is our truck, our family truck. We're going to make money with this truck. In time, we'll have our own business. Now I'll be able to take on larger contracting jobs."

"I meant that the truck is older than I am, and it looks older than any truck I've seen. Whoo! And it still runs?" Joey asked.

"You better believe it does. Our truck was built for a purpose." Mr. Johnson started to say more, but Mama was calling them to the kitchen. She had piled the dishes with ice cream and lit a candle on top of each dish. She gestured to them to sit down at the round kitchen table. Quickly, she dimmed the kitchen lights. Joey was glad that he hadn't eaten much of Doc's soda. One glance at Mama's face told him that she expected him to participate.

"This is our first private family celebration. Our truck is the beginning of a new vision for this family." She blushed as Franklin kissed her. "So let's make a wish."

Joey closed his eyes. There was so much to wish for. Would a wish make Mrs. Hamlin leave him alone? Would a hundred wishes get him into the gifted class with D.J. and Denise? Would ten thousand wishes make his father stay in Berkeley? Would a billion trillion wishes make his family the way it used to be? He peeped at his mother, Mr. Johnson, and Josie. None of his wishes had anything to do with wanting Mr. Johnson, Josie, or that old truck.

Later that night, Joey lay in bed. He reached for Dog, which his father had bought him for his first birthday. As he clutched Dog, he heard the Airedale terrier whimpering in the kitchen. Poor Josie, he thought. She has to sleep in the kitchen when she's used to sleeping with Mr. Johnson. At the thought of the closed bedroom door at the other end of the hall, Joey hit his pillow. That bedroom was off-limits to him as well. No more running in to snuggle with his mother. No more hide-and-seek. He was as locked out as Josie.

Joey got up and eased his bedroom door shut so that he did not have to hear Josie cry. Outside his window, the 1953 Chevrolet pickup truck stood under the moon and stars like a war-horse resting before battle. Joey raised the window and scanned the sky. He saw the lights of an airplane. He wondered if his father was on that plane. He shut the window and reached for Dog, turning away from the door, away from the faint cries that came from the kitchen.

3

The next morning, the two boys angled their bikes across an intersection not far from school.

"Oh, no! I left the note from Mrs. Hamlin at home!" Joey screeched to an abrupt halt.

"Hey, you're going to get us killed!" yelled D.J., biking to the curb. "You want to get it? I'll go with you."

"No, what's the difference? Mrs. Hamlin will punish me if I don't have the note, and she'll punish me if I have the note and I'm late. No use getting you into trouble, D.J." Joey started pedaling.

"But today is Friday, Joey. You know how crazy Fridays are. Come on, let's turn back." D.J. wheeled around and took off. Reluctantly, Joey followed.

Somehow they managed to arrive at the classroom door just before the tardy bell rang. D.J. shoved Joey into the room ahead of him and shut the door. Mrs. Hamlin wasn't even there.

"So here's Mr. Big Mouth." Clark sat on the edge of Joey's desk, his arms folded across his chest. "I've been thinking about that mouthing off you did yesterday. Are you ready to back it up?"

"He was talking to me, too," declared Anthony, mimicking Clark's stance.

Joey gulped. The last thing he needed was to fight Clark and Anthony. They ganged up on anyone they didn't like. D.J. stood next to him. Joey knew that D.J. had never been in a fight in his life.

Clark and Anthony were creating a sensation. Classmates were gathering around them. Even Denise.

"I was talking to whoever tripped me," announced Joey, holding his ground. "If that's you, Anthony, then I was talking to you." The last words came out in one breath, and immediately Joey realized he felt scared.

The two boys edged closer to Joey and D.J. Joey readied himself for a fight. Just then the door opened.

"Well, for once it's quiet in this room. Oh, I see why," said Mrs. Hamlin. "What's going on here?" She stared at Joey.

Clark and Anthony snickered. Clark spoke: "Nothing, Mrs. Hamlin." He and Anthony sauntered to their seats.

"Joey, where's that note? And don't give me any excuses about forgetting it." She showed no reaction when Joey placed his mother's response in her hand.

During recess and lunch, Joey avoided Clark and Anthony. When he returned to the classroom, he saw a large box with several smaller ones in front of the room. Mrs. Hamlin was crouched over the large one. With an expression of distaste on her face, she examined its contents.

"What's that, Mrs. Hamlin?"

"Some new science curriculum that the district is piloting." She scowled. "It has to be set up right away so that these things don't die. What will they think of next? I can't teach everything I'm required to teach now. And they add this."

Joey went up and carefully lifted a container. Grubs moved about inside. Another clear container held two frogs. In another he saw grasshoppers.

"Grasshoppers! Mrs. Hamlin, did you know that they can jump over things five hundred times longer than they are?"

"They aren't going to be jumping anywhere except in that terrarium," Mrs. Hamlin replied, wrinkling her nose.

Joey examined the rest of the science kit. Fascinated, he reached for one of the books stacked beside the large box. This was wonderful! A whole science curriculum with a variety of live organisms! Joey opened the instruction booklet and read. It was easy to identify the parts of the food chain.

"This is great. I can organize this, Mrs. Hamlin," he said. "I know how. I was the science leader in Miss Alder's room. She'll tell you that I'm the best."

"Joey, you can't get your homework in on time or pay attention. How can I trust you to handle this?" With a wide gesture, she dismissed him.

"But, Mrs. Hamlin, please let me. I'll finish all my homework on time. I promise," he begged. "I know how to do this. I'm really smart in natural science. Give me a chance."

She ignored Joey. "Alexander and Sharon, come up here. Joey, thank you, but you need to concentrate on the basics. Take your seat."

Joey watched two of the kids who went to gifted class unload the boxes under Mrs. Hamlin's direction. As Alexander Chang and Sharon Mueller struggled, Joey bit his lip. Seeing Clark and Anthony grin and give each other the thumbs-up sign made him feel worse.

"Hey, Joey, don't let her get to you," D.J. said. "Those two don't know anything about science. Let them mess it up. She'll beg you to help. Wait and see."

Denise pushed a note his way. He balled it up. Clark

mouthed the word *dummy* at Joey. That plus seeing the mocking look on Clark's face was too much. Joey kicked Clark hard under the table. The lanky boy leaped up. Joey threw himself into Clark's fists. They fought.

Kids cheered and screamed. Mrs. Hamlin yelled. D.J. struggled to pull Clark off Joey. Anthony jumped in and hit D.J. As Joey concentrated on giving Clark a punch for every one he got, he heard Denise shouting, "Bugs! Bugs! The bugs are out!"

The classroom door flew open. Miss Alder ran in with another teacher. They pulled the boys apart. Then a petite woman walked in. She uttered one word: "Quiet!" The four boys froze in place. Children scattered to their seats. Grasshoppers hopped from one end of the room to the other. Beetles fanned out everywhere. Alexander and Sharon scurried after them.

Mrs. Mack, the principal of the school, stood by the door. In a low, cool voice she spoke. "Thank you, Miss Alder and Mr. Jeffries, for your assistance. You four young men, march to the front of the room and face the blackboard. Not a word out of you. Class, take a book out and read. Mrs. Hamlin, may I see you outside?"

"Heads down! Lights out!" Mrs. Hamlin said, her voice loud and harsh compared to Mrs. Mack's. About seven minutes later, she returned, lips tight. "All of you boys, go to the office. Now! Alexander and Sharon, get some help and get these grasshoppers and beetles up! The rest of you stay where you are!"

Mrs. Mack was waiting by the stairs. Joey led the group, with D.J. right behind, wiping at his nose. Once in the principal's office, Joey sat as far away from Clark and Anthony as possible. Silently Mrs. Mack handed them each a pad of paper and a sharpened number two pencil with a new eraser. Everyone knew the procedure except D.J. Mrs. Mack had to tell him what to do.

Joey began writing his version of the fight, leaving nothing out. Only the sound of the ticking clock could be heard. Mrs. Mack sat at her desk, her cinnamon-colored hands folded. Silently she collected the pads and read each one, eyeing the writer before turning to the next story.

"Joey, you kicked Clark after he called you a dummy. Clark, you called Joey this name and then hit him. D.J., you went to Joey's aid. Anthony, you jumped on D.J. My. My. My. My." She directed the word at each boy, like a judge handing down a stiff one-syllable sentence.

From the pit of his stomach, Joey felt the bile rise until he could taste it. There was no way he could escape this. No way. D.J. twisted his hands, his eyes shining with tears. Even Clark and Anthony scrunched low in their seats.

Ten minutes later, the four boys were escorted back to their room by a messenger. All four had notes to take home and a serious threat. Joey and Clark had been warned: One more fight and they faced suspension. Joey knew that Mrs. Mack meant it. She was tougher than a tank.

When the bell rang, ending the tumultuous Friday afternoon, Joey trailed behind D.J. to the bike rack. "You want to stop by Doc's? I'll treat you to a Feel Better soda."

D.J. secured his book bag and got onto his bicycle. He started off, then braked. "Nothing will make me feel better. My parents will go nuts when they see this," said D.J., his eyes bleak. "This is the first time I ever got a note. I can't believe it."

"Come on, D.J. I never got notes before this year. Look, I'll call your parents and explain what happened. I promise," Joey said, facing his friend.

"You don't understand. They expect nothing but the best from me. You know what my Dad always says."

" 'D.J.'s going to be the first man in this family to get a college education. He's going to be a neurosurgeon,' " replied Joey, managing to capture the solemn tone of D.J.'s father's voice. Then he rolled his eyes and made his chest expand. " 'Now, isn't that correct, Son. Understand, this is not a question; a simple nod will suffice.' "

In spite of himself, D.J. had to chuckle. Joey joined in. D.J.'s father had big plans for his only son. That thought made Joey pause. His buddy was lucky. D.J. wasn't trapped between anybody.

When they reached the corner where they parted, Joey vowed again to call and talk to D.J.'s parents. Then D.J. took off. Joey headed straight home.

Ernestine's Palace of Beauty was jammed. Joey entered the front door of the shop, a converted two-bedroom apartment, and parked his bike behind the door. Walls had been knocked down to create a spacious room large enough to hold three sinks for washing hair, four hair dryers, and four beautician's stations.

Georgia's manicure table was located near the front window, dwarfed by a philodendron and a hanging Boston fern. A storage room, bathroom, and kitchen in the rear completed the layout. Joey spied his mother at a sink, towel-drying Mrs. Buchanan's hair.

"There's my man!" said Georgia, an almond-colored woman with beaded auburn braids piled on top of her head.

"Did you knock them out at school today?" Georgia thanked her customer, pocketed the tip, and walked toward Joey.

Joey managed to smile, wondering if Georgia knew how appropriate her question was. When she leaned over and kissed his cheek, he was enveloped in the heady perfume she wore. He noticed her nails, long and fire-engine red, with glitter and gold stars. Georgia had worked for Mama since she opened the shop, some six years ago. He liked her.

"Hi, Georgia. You got any errands you want me to run?" asked Joey.

"Not today," she replied. "This is the most honest boy in the world. Right, Ernestine? I mean, you sure raised a fine boy here, girl. Did I ever tell you all about the time I lost my wallet with my birthday money in it? Over a hundred dollars! I was fit to be tied, hunting from one end of this shop to another like a hungry bear. Just when I was ready to collapse, Joey found my wallet. It had fallen behind the magazine rack over there by the coats. He wouldn't even accept a reward, told me it was his birthday present to me. Now, tell me, isn't that too much!"

She laughed. "This child saved my birthday, and did I ever party that night. Believe me, I partied hearty!"

The women in the shop gazed at Joey with approval. Soon they resumed their conversations. Joey watched his mother direct Mrs. Buchanan to the black chair before the lighted mirror, hand her a magazine, and arrange her tools. Her slender hands moved with grace and ease. Everything his mother did, she did that way. But when she turned her eyes on him, he blinked. It was as if a searchlight had discovered him hidden among the rocks.

"Wasn't that good a day at school, was it?" Mama's voice was low. "Want to talk about it? I got a phone call from Mrs. Mack."

He shook his head. In the background he heard Josie barking. Mr. Johnson's dog must be thirsty or lonely. Joey started toward the back door, but the firm hand on his shoulder stopped him in midstep.

"Can we talk later, Mama?" he pleaded. "In private." He saw the tightness in her full lips, the way she tossed her shoulder-length hair, and the telltale arch of her right eyebrow.

Mrs. Buchanan was hanging on to every word. She always did. Soon Mama would have her hair rolled around little bright-pink curlers.

Joey hoped that his mother would agree to hold off. He recognized the tired, tense lines around her eyes.

"All right. We can discuss this later."

Grateful, Joey grabbed his bike. As he left the shop, he remembered how Fridays used to be when Daddy lived with them.

On Fridays, he would hurry home to run errands, get supplies, and sweep the shop floor. The bulk of Mama's customers came on Fridays and Saturdays, so that was when she needed him most. And all those tips, he thought. By Saturday night I'd have pockets stuffed with quarters and dimes. But not anymore. Now I have to study. Mama won't let me work like I used to, until I improve my grades.

Joey opened the gate, locked it, parked his bike, and sat on the back porch. He watched the sturdy Airedale terrier amble over to him. He wondered if she felt as lonely as she looked. From what he'd read about dogs, it was clear that they had feelings. Maybe not feelings like humans, but dog feelings, Joey thought.

Joey settled back against the steps, remembering, hearing his father ring the door buzzer four long times and stride in, brimming over with laughter and life. In his mind he saw his father scoop him up. Off they'd go to get pizza or Chinese food, despite his mother's protests, always despite his mother's protests. And then later, after dinner, after he'd gone to bed, from his bedroom he would hear the voices of two angry people, shouting hurting words. Joey recalled the ones about money and bills and credit cards and being patient. The arguments increased, and the happy times dwindled.

Joey could see his father coming home, more than once, furious because someone *he* had trained had been promoted over him to a managerial position. "They keep passing me over," he would shout. "If I'm good enough to train a manager to run an automobile claims department, then why can't I even interview to be a manager? Ernestine, you know why!"

Joey kept hearing his mother murmuring soothing words, trying to calm Daddy down. But Daddy rolled on like a freight train.

"They won't appoint me to the position I've earned. Why? I'm an African-American man! I'd be the first one. They can't have an African-American man in charge."

Joey squeezed his eyes, hearing Mama trying to comfort his father. "Sugar, they have to give you a promotion soon. You're the best. It will happen; give it time."

Then Daddy would yell, "How much time, Ernestine?

Three hundred more years? I've had it!" And out the door Daddy would go, slamming it.

Without thinking, Joey cupped his hands against his ears, just the way he used to, and shut his eyes as he remembered his mother weeping by the front door. He began to cry, making a muffled, choking sound.

Unexpectedly, against his knee he felt something warm, large and warm. Josie. He reached down and rubbed her back, relieved when she nestled her head against him. Tears fell onto his jeans.

"Josie, I never thought they'd divorce. Why couldn't they stay together? Those people were wrong. Daddy would be a great manager. He was right; I wouldn't let anybody treat me like that. So, why can't Daddy and Mama make up and be a family again? Then life could be the way it used to be, Josie. You'd be with Mr. Johnson, just the two of you." Josie barked and wagged her tail.

Joey opened his eyes and was taken aback by the sight of the overwhelmingly solid pickup truck. In the daylight it looked different. Bigger. Stronger. Uglier. Everything else in the yard seemed small against the bulk of the 1953 Chevy. Joey frowned. His father wouldn't be caught dead in anything except a sharp-looking sports car. But not Mr. Johnson—to him that old truck was the stuff of dreams.

Joey stood. Josie trotted over to the gate and plopped down in front of it, her nose against the metal wire. Joey checked to make sure it was locked. Mr. Johnson was afraid that Josie might get out and not be able to find her way back home or, worse, get hurt. The gate lock was in place.

By the time the moon came out, Joey had finished his

social studies homework and gone down to sweep the beauty-shop floor for Mama. Then he'd fed Josie. A furtive phone call to his father's apartment had resulted in nothing, just the answering machine. I guess Daddy's still in Chicago. I hope he doesn't move. Please, God, don't let him get the job in Chicago.

Mr. Johnson worked late on Friday nights, earning time and a half. As usual, Josie lay before the front door, expecting his key to turn in the lock.

Mama came in a little late, too. Eager to avoid her questions, Joey took the steps two at a time and shut his bedroom door. He was so engrossed in Nintendo, maneuvering his way to the fifth level for the chest of gold, that he jumped when his mother came to sit next to him on the bed. The second he turned toward her, he grimaced. He had forgotten to make the phone call to D.J.'s parents.

Mama reached out and clasped Joey to her. Surprised, he flinched, then relaxed, loving the feel of her arms around him. When she released him, Joey clung to her, then let go.

"So, what happened with you and Mrs. Hamlin today?"

Joey pushed the buttons to end the Nintendo game. He faced his mother. With her, it was better to get the whole story out without stopping or stammering.

"Mrs. Hamlin wouldn't let me set up the new science kit even though I told her I knew how to do it. She chose two kids who go to gifted and told me I had to stick to the basics. Then I got back to my seat and Clark called me a dummy. So I kicked him and we got into a fight and Anthony jumped in to beat me up and D.J. got in to help me, and then the bugs all got out, and the principal and Miss Alder and another teacher came in and Mrs. Mack took all four of us to the office. And I'll get put on suspension if there's any more trouble." He took a deep breath and let it out. "That's all, Mama."

"How can that be all, Joey? What's going on with you? Every week, almost every day, something happens, and it's always bad. You never got into this kind of trouble before—" The last word landed between the two of them like a grenade.

"Before Daddy left and you two got a divorce and you got married to Mr. Johnson," Joey said. "What if Daddy moves to Chicago? I might never see him again. Never."

Mama twisted her hands as if she were trying to scrape something off. She moved over to the window that looked out over the backyard. "I love you, Joey, more than anything. And I love Franklin. I know that the three of us can build a family as strong and solid as that old Chevy out there. And that family includes your father. Can't you see that?" She paused. "Your father and I are your first family and we both love you. So do your grandparents, even though they live in New York and Georgia."

"But what about Daddy living with us? I love Daddy, Mama. Don't you love him anymore?" Joey held his breath. He had never asked her this.

"Not like I used to. I'll always have feelings for him because we share you, Joey. But our marriage couldn't work. For many reasons that are complicated and sad." She sighed. "I don't want you to forget your father. I don't want to do anything to upset your relationship with him. But when I decided to marry Franklin, I made a commitment to build a new family," said his mother, her hands twisting more and more furiously, "and I need your support to do that. I need you to try harder, Joey. Franklin is a good man who cares about you."

"I don't want a new family, Mama. I want our old family, you and me and Daddy," Joey pleaded. He saw that his mother was crying. "Please don't cry, Mama."

"Oh, Joey, I don't know what to do. Why won't you understand that we can't ever have the old family back? You get to see your father and spend time with him. All I'm asking is for you to give our new family a chance. At least give Franklin a chance—let him in. Joey . . ." She held out her arms to him, but he backed away.

"What if Daddy moves to Chicago?" he whispered.

"Then we'll send you to visit him and you'll write him and talk on the phone, or if that doesn't—" She stopped, aware of the sounds of steps on the stairs. They had been too involved to hear Josie's welcoming barks.

"Or what, Mama?" persisted Joey, not caring if Mr. Johnson heard or not. His mother didn't reply right away.

"Or if living here makes you too unhappy, we'll see about your living with your daddy for a while." His mother walked over to the doorway, where Mr. Johnson now stood. "Franklin, Joey got into trouble in school again. A fight this time. Nothing is getting any better. I don't know what to do anymore." The tears slid down her cheeks. She brushed past her husband and ran into their bedroom.

Mr. Johnson leaned against the door frame. Josie jumped up, barking, trying to get his attention. "I'm going to go in and talk to your mother. I brought home a large pizza with all the extras you like on it. Go on downstairs and set the table," he said. He continued to pat his dog.

Joey waited for Mr. Johnson to get mad at him. He'd never

seen his stepfather really angry. Joey's insides churned. Seeing his mother cry like that hurt. It hurt even more to know that he had made her cry. But he felt bad, too. Bad and mad. Joey stared at his shoelaces.

Mr. Johnson started down the hall and then came back. "By the way, Joey, who did you get into a fight with?"

"Clark. And then Anthony jumped in."

"Why did you boys fight?"

"Clark called me a dummy." Joey thrust his hands into his jeans pockets.

"That was a dumb thing for him to say, 'cause you're nobody's dummy. Who won, anyway?" Mr. Johnson smiled, making his eyes squint together.

In spite of himself, Joey smiled back. "I got some pretty good hits in."

Mr. Johnson nodded as if answering a question he had asked himself. "Set that table, and if you're hungry, go on and start eating. I may be with your mama for a while. Let Josie out for me. We are going to have to start working this out, Joey. I can't stand to see Ernestine unhappy." He left.

Joey watched Mr. Johnson's straight back, solid as an oak door. Then he blurted out, "You wish I'd go live with Daddy and then it would be just you and my mama."

Mr. Johnson stopped. With deliberate steps he headed back toward Joey. For several seconds nothing happened. Then he spoke.

"I spent my whole life growing up without a family. I lived in foster homes. Never belonging. So I know how you feel. Scared. Furious. Mixed-up." He paused. "Joey, you have a family. I want this marriage to work. I've got a lot riding on it. This is my first family, ever."

Joey looked at Mr. Johnson. Doc's talk echoed in his head, and he thought, All of us—me, Mama, Mr. Johnson, Daddy, even Josie—are going through changes. But they already chose their doors. What am I going to do?

"One more thing, Joey. I don't want you to go away. I want to help you. But you have to let me."

Joey stared in amazement as Mr. Johnson walked to the closed door at the opposite end of the hallway. How could he never have had a real family? he wondered. Mama never told him about this. Where were Mr. Johnson's father and mother? Well, at least I know one thing: Mr. Johnson is here to stay.

When Joey saw the large pizza sitting on the chair by the door, he couldn't help thinking about his father. But his father wasn't in the ktichen singing. His father hadn't bought the pizza. They wouldn't be making a crazy salad tonight with his daddy tossing in leftover vegetables and even fruit. No, his father would not be coming home.

He wondered if Mama and Mr. Johnson would send him to Chicago to live with his father. Somehow the thought of that didn't make him feel better. A check upstairs confirmed that his mother's bedroom door remained shut. Doc had talked about choosing doors. But how can I choose anything? Everything keeps shutting down all around me.

Then the promise that he had made to D.J. came to his mind. His head throbbed. How can things get any worse than this? Joey asked himself as he lifted the pizza box and headed for the kitchen, with Josie plodding behind him. He had to call D.J.'s parents and try to convince them not to punish his friend.

4

Joey watched as Mr. Johnson hoisted two cans of paint onto the back of the battered pickup truck. He yawned. Calling D.J.'s parents hadn't been easy. Nothing he said had seemed to lessen the shock in D.J.'s mother's voice. His father had been even harder. In his head, Joey replayed the lengthy lecture he'd endured about acting mature and behaving with dignity and common sense. Finally they had let him go. Unable to stop himself, Joey yawned again.

His mother and Mr. Johnson must have come down after he'd eaten four slices of pizza and gone to bed. Not even his library of books about animal life had interested him. He'd gone straight to bed. Throughout the night he had awakened and tiptoed to the telephone, thinking that he had heard it ring, but he hadn't.

In the chilly October morning air, Joey stood by his bicycle near the porch. High above him the first snatches of fog had started to separate and burn away, leaving spots of sky behind. He hoped that eventually the sun would shine.

Other than a greeting, Mr. Johnson had not uttered a word. At last he closed the scarred back of the truck and turned to Joey. "Joey, you're welcome to go with me today, same as last weekend," Mr. Johnson offered. His deep-set eyes were fixed on Joey. "This week we've got the truck; makes a real difference. I got some jobs I could use your help with."

"No." Joey hurried to add, "I mean, I can't go. I have to stay here and help Mama, Mr. Johnson. And I got homework to do, sir." The word spilled over one another.

Mr. Johnson sighed. For a moment sadness gripped his mouth. Joey knew that expression. Every time he said "Mr. Johnson" or "sir," his stepfather got that look. But Joey couldn't figure out what to call him.

"I won't make you come, Joey. I would like you to, though. Tell your mama that I'll do my best to get home early tonight." Mr. Johnson stared at Joey hard before he closed the truck door. Josie barked her happy yelps from the front seat.

Joey tracked the old truck until it rounded the corner. He kicked the front tire of his bike. From the beauty shop, he heard Gladys and Susie bantering back and forth. Somewhere inside he knew that his mother was working hard. She'd been down there since 6:00 A.M., taking early customers.

"Good morning, Joey!" A woman waved and entered Ernestine's Palace of Beauty. Joey sat on the porch, trying to decide what to do next.

More women arrived, until the shop sang out with laughter and chatter. All day long women would come to get their hair pressed, curled, permed, relaxed, braided, extended, trimmed, cut, streaked, tinted, or dyed.

When Georgia strolled past him, beaming, he heard his mother say, "About time you got here, girl." Being late was about the only thing Georgia did with regularity. The next words that rang out had a jagged edge: "Joey Davis, I need to talk to you."

Mama's mad at me. Might have been smarter to go with Mr. Johnson, he reflected. Joey wheeled the bike into the beauty shop, rested it against the wall by the door, and jammed his hands into his jacket pockets. The familiar smells spun around his head. Exotic perfumes and oils and creams. Strong coffee perking. Sweet rolls from the bakery down the street.

"There's that fine boy of yours, Ernestine," Gladys teased. "Don't you ever feed him?"

"All day long," his mother answered. But the smile on her lips did not match the disapproval in her eyes.

"That's one good kid you got there, honey. And honest, too." Georgia was getting ready to start in on that old lost wallet story.

But Joey's mother intervened. "Well, maybe I'll keep him," she said, combing out the curls in Mrs. Lewis's white hair. The elderly woman had recently retired. Joey knew her well. She had been his kindergarten teacher.

"And one of these days, Joey, you might have a little brother or sister," said Mrs. Lewis. "Now, wouldn't that be nice? Then you wouldn't have to be so lonely. You'd have someone to play with and be responsible for. Nothing like having brothers and sisters, that's what I say."

Joey retorted, "I'm not lonely and I have lots of friends to play with."

Mrs. Lewis adjusted her glasses, ignoring him. "Ernestine, anybody who has a child as smart as this one should have two or three children. We need smart children. And you're a very young woman. Wouldn't a little one be wonderful?"

Joey frowned again. Why did Mrs. Lewis keep talking about his mama having a baby? They didn't need a baby. Anyway, it was none of her business.

"There's plenty of time before Franklin and I think about doing that, Mrs. Lewis, but that was kind of you to say. We're not planning on adding to our family any time soon." Mama turned to Joey. "I hoped you would be going out in the truck this morning with Franklin."

Joey counted the squares on the clean linoleum floor.

"So, talk to me. Franklin told me that he was going to ask you again." She pursed her lips.

"I told him I couldn't go, Mama."

"Why not? You don't work here like you used to. You know that. Why won't you give Franklin a chance? Why won't you try?" she pressed.

"Mama, I've got a lot to do today. Homework. I promised D.J. I'd come over." Joey begged with his eyes, praying that his mother wouldn't embarrass him in front of everyone.

"Oh, Son, Franklin planned a special day for the two of you."

"Mr. Johnson didn't tell me that." Seeing the expression on her face when he said "Mr. Johnson" made Joey waver. He did not want to make her cry again. "Okay, I'll go with him next Saturday. I promise, Mama." With that, Joey dashed to the door and grabbed the handlebars of his bicycle.

"Joey, why do you insist on calling Franklin 'Mr. Johnson'? He's your stepfather, not some stranger."

Joey fled before she could say more. He hurled himself onto his bike and headed down the street toward D.J.'s home. But in his heart he still heard the hurt in his mother's questions and saw Mr. Johnson's face when he had refused to go.

"What do they expect me to do? How am I supposed to act?" Joey dodged around a girl. "A baby? I'm glad Mama isn't planning on having a baby anytime soon. What a change that would be." He lowered his head against the wind and pedaled faster.

Two blocks down and four blocks over, Joey squeezed his brakes in front of a white stucco apartment building. He idled there, wondering if D.J. would even want to see him. Deciding to take the risk, Joey wrestled his bike up two flights of stairs. He was both relieved and anxious when his friend answered the door.

"Hi, D.J., can I come in?" he asked.

D.J. stood there, silent and stern-faced.

"Look, I'm really sorry. I did my best to explain everything to your parents. I took all the blame," pleaded Joey.

Unexpectedly, D.J. waved him in. "Get in here, you 'potentially dangerous and distracting influence,' " D.J. said with a teasing grin.

"Me?" asked Joey.

"That's what Dad said about you. Don't worry. Thanks for calling. They both yelled at me for an hour and then gave me the lecture about 'being a role model for our race.' " D.J. shook his head. "Mama's at some church committee meeting and Dad's asleep."

D.J.'s father worked the night shift at a hospital. Gratefully, Joey skirted D.J.'s sisters, imagining, as he always did, what it would be like to have to live with five sisters. D.J. seemed to handle it just fine.

The large, clean kitchen was empty. Sunlight poured in. Joey leaned against a counter.

"D.J., why do you think Mrs. Hamlin hates me?"

D.J. placed some food on the table. "I don't think she hates you. I think she just doesn't like teaching."

Joey reached for an apple and bit into it. "Then why'd she become a teacher?"

D.J. shrugged. "Who knows? Maybe she thought it would be different. Maybe she sees that she made a mistake and that's what makes her so angry."

"I know about feeling angry," replied Joey.

"I'll testify to that. Want a sandwich?" D.J. offered.

After a breakfast of peanut-butter-and-strawberry-jelly sandwiches, popcorn, and two scoops each of rocky road ice cream, they took off. D.J. led, keeping to streets within five miles of where they lived. Past wood-framed houses, stucco apartment buildings, corner stores, the post office, parks, around buses, cars, vans, and through side streets, the boys whizzed.

Wind currents sailed past Joey's head. Every now and then D.J. would holler something back to him. But mostly they rode. Joey tried to push the earlier part of the morning behind him, but he couldn't. He kept seeing the sturdy Chevrolet pickup truck drive off. He tried to picture what Mr. Johnson was doing now. Lost in his thoughts, he barely heard a horn honking to his left. D.J. yelled back at him. Almost without thinking, he stopped.

"Kid! Watch where you're going!" a man shouted at him from a car. Joey looked. Next to the man was a boy almost his age.

"Sorry," Joey muttered, flushed. The man pulled away. Joey heard him telling the boy, "Now, Son, when you're on your bike, be more careful."

"Man, you almost got hit," D.J. said. "We should take a break. There's a store over there. I'm thirsty."

Joey followed D.J. to the corner store, and they parked

their bikes where they could see them. Instead of going in, Joey dug money out of his jeans pocket and waited.

D.J.'s round, brown eyes bore into Joey like an electric drill. "So what's the matter with you? You never did anything like that before," he said.

"Nothing."

"Come on! This is major. If that man hadn't seen you, he would have hit you. Didn't you notice him pulling out of that parking space?" asked D.J.

"My mind was on something else. I'm not a ghost crab with 360-degree vision," retorted Joey, more shaken than angry.

For a minute or so, D.J. clenched his hands. "First, how can anything see all around at the same time? Second, did your dad call yet?" he asked.

"The ghost crab has two tall stalks on top of its head. Instead of sitting on top of the stalks, the eyes surround them. And the answer to your second question is no, but I know Daddy is going to. He's just busy," Joey explained.

"Did your new dad take you out in the truck yet?"

"He's not my new dad!" Joey yelled. "I got a daddy. My own. A real one. Mr. Johnson is not my father!"

"Okay. Okay. Why are you so angry all the time? No matter what happens, you end up angry and in trouble. Look, I keep telling you, having a stepfather isn't so bad," D.J. said. "He's a nice man. Better than not having anyone."

Joey considered that. Why didn't his best friend understand that it wasn't that he hated Mr. Johnson? In fact, it was hard to have any bad feelings toward Mr. Johnson as a person. Mr. Johnson didn't hit him or even yell like his father used to. It was just that he wanted Daddy home again and that meant that Mr. Johnson couldn't stay. But how could he make him move out? The sight of his mother crying tore Joey apart. That was one thing he and Mr. Johnson had in common—seeing Mama unhappy upset both of them.

"You don't get it, D.J. Mr. Johnson will never be my father."

"I did not mean that and you know it," D.J. replied, his round face sober. "But he can be your friend. I know this is a tough time for you, but you've got to do something about being mad all the time. Give the man a break, Joey. Why can't you have your father and him, too?"

"That's what Mama keeps telling me. You think I like feeling mad all the time? I hate it! But I don't know what to do, D.J. I miss Daddy, and having Mr. Johnson living in the house feels wrong. I try. But I—oh, I don't know." He threw up his hands.

Feeling all mixed-up, Joey drifted around the aisles, past unpacked boxes. He had almost five dollars, but he wasn't hungry, even though it was nearly lunchtime. He moved past the ice-cream cartons and Popsicles. As he walked around a carton of dried-soup boxes, he stopped in front of a shelf with cupcakes. Without thinking, not even bothering to glance around, as if from a great height he watched his left hand reach out. He stared as he picked up a package of cupcakes. His heart beating against his chest, he crammed the two chocolate cream-filled cupcakes into his jacket pocket.

At that moment, D.J. bounded up. In one hand he held a can of soda and a sandwich. "You getting anything?" he asked. A package of potato chips and a candy bar were clutched in his other hand.

Joey stiffened. More than anything he wanted to pull the cupcakes out of their hiding place. Put them back. Pay for them. Anything. Just get them out of his pocket. More than anything he wanted to ask D.J. to help him. But he couldn't. Like an animal caught in the blazing headlights of a big-rig truck, he froze.

"You deaf or something? What are you going to buy?" D.J. shifted his weight from one foot to the other.

"Hey, are you boys buying anything?" yelled the clerk behind the counter at the front of the store.

"Come on. I don't want to get into any more trouble," D.J. said and walked down the aisle. "Come on, Joey!" He grabbed Joey's arm and tugged him along.

Joey's hands dangled at his side. Mute, he followed his friend to the counter. It was too late to take the cupcakes out. Too late. The clerk might see. A terrifying thought snaked into Joey's mind. Maybe the clerk had seen him steal the cupcakes. He could still pay for them. But he couldn't figure out how to get them out of his pocket without getting caught.

He darted a quick look at the clerk's face. The young man was punching the buttons on an old cash register as D.J. counted out his money.

"Hey, kid, what are you buying?" The man leaned across the counter. "What's the matter with your friend?" he asked D.J.

D.J. shrugged.

"Nothing's wrong," Joey stammered. "I'm not hungry. My stomach hurts."

The man watched him. Joey held his breath. Then the

clerk reached into his shirt pocket and took out a package of Life Savers. He peeled back the covering and pointed the package at Joey.

"Here, you don't look so good. Take one," he said.

Joey took an orange Life Saver and put it in his mouth. The candy sat on his tongue like a smooth pebble.

"Thanks," he said. He wanted to erase the last few minutes and return to the second when he'd entered the store. He wanted to watch the cupcakes float back to their place on the shelf, unseen by anyone except him. But it was too late.

"Come on, I'll share my sandwich with you," D.J. offered.

Barely able to see before him, Joey left the store. He waited for the touch of the clerk's hand on his shoulder. But nothing happened. Nothing. Cars drove past. People strolled by. The cool bay breeze blew in from the Pacific Ocean. Daring a glance back, Joey saw the clerk reading a magazine.

"Hey, let's go sit over there. I'm starved." D.J. climbed onto his bike and took off to the park across the street. Joey's arm brushed up against the cupcakes as he gripped his handlebars.

As soon as he could, he got away, telling D.J. that he felt sick and had to get home. For the rest of the afternoon Joey rode around in a blur. Twice he biked near the corner store and slowed down. But he couldn't force himself to go inside. So he headed for Doc's drugstore.

The clocks were ticking and bonging and cuckooing. Bold notes from a trumpet solo flowed through the chatter. There was a line at the front counter, and all six stools at the soda fountain were filled. Doc was glowering at the cash register. "Joey! I need your help. Quick, you know how to handle the cash register. Take care of this customer while I go and make Ed his tuna-and-egg-salad sandwich." Doc patted his shoulder.

Doc was right. He did know which buttons to push and how to use the hand-held computer to make change. He could even read the tax chart. Joey shoved his jacket under the counter. When his hand touched the jacket pocket, he felt sick, but he shook it off and began to ring up toothpaste, a movie magazine, and a birthday card. Doc only accepted cash, unless you were on his list of special customers. Fortunately, only cash customers came up during the next hour.

Joey concentrated on ringing up the purchases, making change, and bagging. Working in Doc's store was much more fun than helping Mama in the beauty shop. Here he felt grown-up, not like Ernestine's little boy who needed a baby sister or brother. Slamming the cash door shut, pushing the lever that snapped it open, accepting the dollar bills and coins, sorting them into the right compartments, and tearing off the receipts were his kind of work. He heard himself whistling. Doc was right. Working made him feel better, less angry and confused. Wouldn't it be great if I could work here? Maybe Mama would let me, he thought.

A plan formed in his head as he realized that the line had ended. Maybe Mr. Johnson would speak up for me. Or if I went out on the truck with him, maybe Mama would give in. But how could he help Mama, go out with Mr. Johnson, satisfy the impossible Mrs. Hamlin, duck Clark and Anthony, and try to get into gifted class? Not even a silkworm moth with its eleven brains could figure this out for me, he thought. Or do something about the cupcakes.

Doc waved him over and pointed to an empty stool. On

the plate in front of him, Joey saw a turkey sandwich and chips. Hungry, he ate. But when it was time for him to leave, he didn't want to go. As he bent to get his jacket, the package of cupcakes almost tumbled out. Aware of Doc's eyes on him, Joey straightened up. Doc respects me, he thought. How can I tell him what I did? He'd never trust me like he did today.

"Hey, Joey. We haven't had time to talk. How are you doing?" Doc asked, wiping down the counter with a damp towel.

"Okay."

"Then why are you looking like the world ended?"

Joey shrugged.

"Well, thanks for your help. That girl I hired to be here during the busy times shows up when she feels like it. Teenagers exist in their own world, somewhere up around Pluto. Too bad I can't find somebody as dependable as you," Doc added.

Now Joey knew he could never confess to Doc that he had stolen a package of cupcakes. And stolen them for no good reason. It wasn't as if he couldn't have bought the cupcakes. Why did I do it? Joey asked himself. Why? Suddenly weary, he left the drugstore.

The darkening sky made Joey shiver as he slowly pedaled his way home. Parked in front of the open garage door was the pickup truck. Joey saw Mr. Johnson moving from the truck into the garage, hauling equipment. He wheeled his bike around, hoping to park it inside the gate and dash to his room. Hunched over, his eyes down, he brushed by the side of the truck. Josie sat near the garage door.

"Joey, give me a hand. Hope your day went better than

mine." Mr. Johnson lifted an aluminum extension ladder and carried it into the garage. "Went by to bid on a job and the customer told me he'd changed his mind, didn't have enough money. Didn't even bother to call me."

Joey waited.

"Grab the paint. You know where it goes. Over there by the side door." Mr. Johnson rested the tall ladder securely against the wall. Joey picked up a can of paint. It was heavy.

Working silently, he and Mr. Johnson unloaded the truck. The garage was arranged by tools. Cabinets and tool chests lined the walls. Mr. Johnson had every drawer labeled. There were bars on the windows and side door. Joey knew that the tools were quite expensive. As he shifted some paint rollers from one hand to the other, he squashed the package of cupcakes. Startled, he dropped the rollers. The clanging noise sounded even louder inside the garage.

"Joey, be careful with those!" Mr. Johnson came over and began picking them up.

Joey bent to help him. Suddenly his stomach clenched. He moaned.

"What's wrong?"

"Sorry, Mr. Johnson." Joey pressed his hand to his stomach, hoping that the burning sensation would stop.

"What's hurting you? Did you eat something?"

"No, I'm okay. Really, Mr. Johnson."

"Don't tell me that. I've been knowing you for almost a year. You don't just look sick. Joey, you look scared. What's wrong?" Mr. Johnson put everything down and led Joey to a workbench.

The awful burning let up. Joey released a breath.

"I just don't feel so good." He sat there on the cold wood,

his hands in his pockets. The stolen cupcakes beneath his fingers felt like two chocolate bricks. He had never shoplifted before. Mama and Daddy would be so ashamed of me if they found out, he thought. And if D.J.'s parents learned about this, they'd never let us be friends.

"Look at me," said Mr. Johnson, sitting beside Joey. He smelled of paint and wood. Joey noticed his rough hands, the knuckles large and spattered with blue paint.

Reluctantly, Joey obeyed.

"Joey, I know the difference between sick and scared to death. You look scared to death, and I want to know why. Maybe I can help." Mr. Johnson touched his arm.

It was weird, because of everyone he knew, Mr. Johnson was the only one who didn't know him well enough to make him feel worse about what he had done. "I just—I didn't mean to—" Stuck, Joey shut his mouth.

"You didn't mean to what?" Mr. Johnson waited. "Look, whatever you did we can talk about. Just us. You don't have to be afraid of me. Now, continue."

Joey took a deep breath. "Mr. Johnson, what if someone does something, something kinda—no, real bad," he said, "but they didn't mean to? Honestly, they didn't mean to." His eyes filled with tears.

Mr. Johnson was quiet. Then he asked, "Did that person hurt anyone?"

"Oh, no!" Joey wiped at his tears. "Not bad like that."

"Did that person get anyone else into trouble?"

Joey thought. "Only that person got into trouble."

"Did that person ever do this bad thing before?"

"Oh, no! Not ever and I'll—I mean, that person will never

do anything bad again. That person needs—" Joey held his head in his hands.

"Needs what?" Mr. Johnson's voice was as soft as black velvet.

"Needs a new day to start over again. Needs a gigantic eraser to wipe out everything that happened today."

"Sounds like that person believes that he is in serious trouble and feels ashamed about whatever he did," said his stepfather.

"Oh, you don't know how bad it is, Mr. Johnson," Joey wailed, looking up. "Nobody could." At that moment, the divorce, Daddy and Chicago, Mrs. Hamlin, school, and all the rest swept over Joey. It wasn't only the cupcakes. But years of his parents' arguments couldn't be used as an excuse. Nothing could. I did this. Me, Joey told himself.

Deep-set, weary, brownish black eyes bore into Joey. Then Mr. Johnson did the last thing Joey expected him to do. He started laughing. Really laughing.

Shocked, Joey asked, "Are you laughing at me?"

"No, no. I am laughing at a boy about thirteen years old who asked his uncle questions like yours about, let me see . . ." Mr. Johnson figured out the time. "About twenty years ago."

Curious, Joey asked, "What was the bad thing that boy did?"

"Oh, now, that's a secret. I don't know if we trust each other well enough for me to tell you. I've only told two people. But I can say this, it was a serious mistake."

"What happened to that boy?" Joey asked.

Mr. Johnson smiled. "That's the best part of the story."

"Did he get in a whole lot of trouble?"

"In one way, but not in another. He had his uncle to help get him on the right road," Mr. Johnson replied. "And to teach him how to become the kind of man who held on to his dreams and worked for them, no matter what."

"He did?"

"You bet he did. My Uncle Mike was great. He wasn't my blood uncle, but he was like kin to me. Uncle Mike was a social worker." Mr. Johnson smiled.

"You were that boy, Mr. Johnson?" Joey wiped his eyes. "You did something bad?"

"You could say that. So, Joey, do you want to talk about it now or later?" he asked.

Joey thought a minute. "Maybe later."

"Fine with me. You let me know when."

"Are you going to tell Mama?" Joey dared to ask.

Mr. Johnson stood up, rising above him like the face of a granite cliff. "No, Joey. We had our first talk. A real conversation about an imaginary boy with an imaginary problem. Now, let's get this truck unloaded and lock up. I'm starved."

Without another word, the two of them labored side by side until the equipment was stored and the garage locked. Joey waited for Mr. Johnson to say something else, but he didn't.

When Joey got inside, he found a note on the kitchen table in his mother's handwriting, saying that his father had called. He sprinted to the telephone. It had to be good news. It had to be.

Crossing the fingers of one hand, Joey pushed the buttons

for the long string of numbers. After five rings, his father answered.

"Daddy! When are you coming home?"

"Joey, I wanted you to know that I made it to the final interviews, so I'll be in Chicago until next Wednesday. Maybe longer, if I get this position," replied his father.

"What do you mean?"

"Automobile claims manager for a pretty large area. Exactly what I have always wanted. Marshall Corporation has its headquarters here in Chicago, and, Joey, this is some city! You'll love it. A guy told me about some science museums here that will take us days to tour."

Joey felt the floor beneath him plummet. "Daddy, you mean you might move there? Leave me here? Just go?" The questions sputtered out. "Daddy?"

"Look, son, I don't want to leave you. But it seems that filing that complaint about not even being considered for a promotion grabbed their attention. I'm not invisible anymore. All I've wanted was the opportunity to interview. Just the shot I earned. See, Joey?" his father asked.

Joey squirmed, remembering the years of turmoil. It had gotten worse when Daddy and Mama had started arguing about his father filing a discrimination complaint against Marshall Corporation. Finally, Daddy had shouted at him and Mama, "How can my son learn to fight for his rights if his own father can't? Ernestine, please understand, I have to do this."

A voice brought Joey back. "Son, you still there?"

"Sure, Daddy. I know that you have to interview, but I don't want you to move," he said, sitting down.

"I want you to be proud of me, Son."

Joey protested, "But I am proud of you, Daddy."

"Son, I haven't got the job yet. And if I do get it, I won't be living here forever. You'll be able to fly out and see me whenever you want."

"When will you know, Daddy?"

"By the end of next week. I've got to go now. I've got tons of material to read for the next round of interviews. Wish me luck. Kiss your mother for me. Oh, how are you doing in school? Everything going okay?" his father added.

Joey said, "Sure, Daddy, no problems at all. Everything's great."

"That's my boy. Talk to you soon."

The buzzing of a dead line told Joey that the conversation was over. Tears welled in his eyes. Joey grabbed his jacket and ran upstairs to his room. He collapsed on the bed. Minutes later, he heard a soft plop-plop sound. Raising his head, he saw Josie sitting by his door.

"So what are you doing in here? Feeling deserted, too?"

Josie lowered herself and placed her head on her front paws.

"You look as pitiful as me. Josie, what are we going to do? Nobody treats us like they're supposed to. Not Mama. Not Daddy. And for you, not Mr. Johnson."

5

Saturday night was a blur of television programs for Joey. Mr. Johnson made cups of hot cocoa for everyone. Then he lifted Mama's legs onto his lap, removed her shoes, and rubbed her feet. Joey went to bed. The hot milk helped him drift off.

When he woke up Sunday morning, he knew that Mama had let him sleep instead of making him go to church. His plans to hide out in his room ended with a call from Mr. Johnson.

"Joey, up and dressed! I need your help," yelled his stepfather from the backyard.

A half hour later, Joey was following Mr. Johnson from the garage to the side of the house. The truck took up so much room. The battered station wagon had been sold for scrap.

"These gutters and downspouts need cleaning and painting," said his stepfather, propping a ladder against the house. "Hand me that scraper and plastic bag."

"This one?"

"Right. Get the paint and brushes by the truck. I'll show you how to paint the bottom areas. We'll need to replace all the gutters in a few years," said Mr. Johnson, climbing the ladder.

They drove themselves to complete the job by dusk. Joey worked with Mr. Johnson, learning how to properly clean and store the tools.

For dinner, Mama had prepared stuffed baked chicken,

broccoli, and wild rice, with a lemon cake for dessert. Tired but hungry, Joey asked for second helpings.

"The gutters and downspouts look new. I sure am lucky to have you two," said Mama, placing a biscuit on Joey's plate.

Mr. Johnson smiled. Joey blushed. Maybe Doc was right—hard work did ease the hurt.

Later that evening, with his homework completed and checked by Mama, school clothes laid out, and books piled, ready for a week with Mrs. Hamlin, there was nothing left to do except read his nature books. Mama allowed only one hour of Nintendo a night during the school term. Too exhausted to concentrate, Joey crawled into bed. Josie was in the kitchen. Mama and Mr. Johnson were snuggled close on the couch.

Joey's eyes fell on his jacket. The cupcakes were still jammed in the pocket. In one swift movement, Joey crossed the room, removed the cupcakes, and thrust them under the mattress at the top left-hand corner of his bed. The bedroom door was slightly ajar, but Josie did not come in.

Late that night, unable to sleep, Joey heard whimpers from the kitchen. He tiptoed downstairs. The sole sounds in the house came from Josie and the grandfather clock in the hallway. Joey opened the wooden gate that kept Josie locked in. After pouring a glass of milk and getting a handful of peanut butter cookies, Joey sat down on the floor by the Airedale terrier. She didn't move. He offered her part of a cookie. With a delicate tilt of her head, Josie accepted.

"Be glad you're not a flamingo, girl." Joey smiled at Josie. She cocked her head. "Guess what that means. You've got ten seconds."

Josie's ears perked up. She tipped her head to the other side.

"Okay, time's up. I'll tell you why. If you were a flamingo, you would have to grab these cookies with your mouth upside down." Joey handed her more cookie, chuckling to himself. "Flamingos put their large beaks upside down in the water to strain out the dirt and get the food."

The kitchen floor felt hard beneath him, but images of his father flying away into a purplish night filled his head. When Josie laid her head on his left knee, his hand reached out to her.

The week crawled by. By Wednesday the classroom had returned to normal. The insects lived strictly within the confines of their terrariums. Except for minimal maintenance, Mrs. Hamlin ignored the science area. Joey frowned, knowing how exciting it could be if she would let him run it.

"Joey, I want to see you after school," said Mrs. Hamlin, laying literature test results faceup on his desk. Denise gawked. D.J.'s jaw dropped. Clark opened his mouth as if to say something, but settled for a snort. A huge, red F covered the top sheet. Joey read the A on D.J. and Denise's papers and the D-minus on Clark's. He balled the test up and stuffed it into his desk, fuming at himself for not caring enough to try.

After school, with the classroom empty, Joey headed for the terrariums. They needed cleaning. Mrs. Hamlin had escorted the class to the outside door. She might be gone long enough for him to do some work.

Joey studied the procedures in the written material, then began cleaning and reorganizing the science center. Handling the insects wasn't awkward. He knew how to be careful so that none escaped.

Suddenly Joey heard Mrs. Hamlin's voice. "I told you to leave that alone," she said. "I want to talk to you about your grades."

"Please let me finish. It won't take long."

"All right. That mess over there certainly looks better. I've got a report to get in. Every time I turn around there's another report due. If I'd known this was what teaching was like . . ."

D.J. had been right. Joey stiffened inside. He'd spend hundreds of hours with Mrs. Hamlin before school ended in June. It was only October! How could he stand it? One look at her distressed face made him wonder if she could bear it.

Mrs. Hamlin swept a stack of papers aside to clear a small space on her desk. "We'll talk in twenty minutes."

The next twenty minutes became the best Joey had spent in school since being in Miss Alder's room. Humming softly to himself, he worked as the clock ticked. A sweet peace enveloped him.

"Joey, if you are finished, come over here."

"Mrs. Hamlin, don't you want to check what I did?" he asked.

Reluctantly, the teacher walked over and surveyed the neat, clean table with labeled containers. Joey stood back.

"Nothing got out?" she asked, her speech terse and clipped.

"Not one insect."

"Well." She paused. "Very good. This looks better. Now let's talk."

Joey followed her to her desk and sat in a chair near it.

"Your grades are terrible. You seem as if you can't focus when I'm teaching. You have difficulty staying with a task. You have a serious attention deficit and need special help, Joey," Mrs. Hamlin said, speaking to some spot above his right ear.

"Special help? What are you talking about? Nothing's wrong with me," Joey protested.

"There's a special class that you can go to for part of the week. I talked with the teacher and explained the problem to her. But we'll need to meet with your parents and have you tested," she explained, her eyes narrowing. Nervously Mrs. Hamlin combed her hair with her fingers.

"I want to get into the gifted class! Miss Alder said I was smart enough to be in the gifted class like D.J. and Denise. I don't have any problem," Joey argued, standing up. "You don't like me! That's why you're saying this! I know you don't like me."

"What are you getting upset about? Of course I like you, Joey." The teacher directed the last sentence to the ceiling. She cleared her throat. "This special class would make learning easier for you. As for Miss Alder, that was last year. I am your teacher this year. Now, take this note home to your parents."

At the door, Joey stopped, so enraged that he could hardly breathe. "What about Clark? *He* needs special help. Real special help." The words were flung out like a challenge.

"Clark is none of your concern. You are the one with the problem." Mrs. Hamlin turned her back to him.

"No, I'm not! I don't have any learning problem!" Joey shouted, slamming the door behind him. "But you do."

All the way home, Joey's feet felt like bar weights. Instead of going to Ernestine's Palace of Beauty, he biked to Doc's drugstore. Everything was the same: clocks, jazz music, smells, merchandise, and twinkling Christmas lights.

I need Christmas today, Joey thought, searching for Doc. Then he spotted him. Joey went over to the counter.

Doc rang up a sale, then joined Joey on a stool. He ran his hand through his cropped white hair and sighed. For a long time neither of them spoke. Joey wondered which anniversary it was. Doc acted this way only at certain times of the year.

Joey sneaked a look to his right. Sure enough, Doc's eyes stared at a photograph of his wife. Dismayed, Joey noticed the tremor in his friend's hands.

"Joey, do you know what today is?" Without waiting for a response, Doc continued, his voice stronger. "On this day, over forty years ago, I met my wife at a church social. Joey, you talk about one fine-looking, smart-stepping lady, that was my Elizabeth. I miss her every day. I never thought I'd have to live without her." Doc lowered his head.

"Doc, I'm sorry. I really am," said Joey. "Can I do anything?"

Doc lifted his head and shook it from side to side. Then he let out a deep breath. "What am I doing? Here I am talking to you and D.J. about making tough changes. What a hypocrite I am." Doc slapped his head.

"Doc, what do you mean? I don't understand."

"Joey, I need to keep growing, too. Look around you. I need to open the pharmacy back up, hire somebody to work the counter and the rest of the store. Start making some real money. I'll miss Elizabeth the rest of my life. But telling you one thing and doing another makes me a fake," Doc said, gazing back at the closed pharmacy.

"You're no fake, Doc. You're my friend. I trust you."

Doc stood up straighter. "Then I'd better get busy living up to the trust you've placed in me." His voice was stronger, but still sad. Joey remembered a nature story about a male crane whose mate had been killed by a car. The crane had returned to the same exact spot every day for months and months.

Doc moved behind the fountain. He made two chocolate malts and a ham sandwich on rye.

With a malt and half of a thick sandwich in front of him, Joey sighed. "Thanks, Doc. This looks good."

"You came by here for a reason. I could tell the minute I saw your face." Doc listened while Joey told him the whole story about Mrs. Hamlin wanting to put him in a special-education class for part of each school week.

"I don't have any kind of attention deficit. Why listen to her? She can't even teach science. All she does is scream at us." Joey bit into his sandwich.

"No, you don't belong in any special class. Life has been difficult for you since your folks parted ways." Doc sipped his thick malt.

"What should I do? Can she make me go?"

"Let's finish up here and you get on home. Talk to your parents about this. Call your father. Talk to your mother. They'll know what to do," Doc said. "Joey, I am convinced that this critical educational decision, which could affect the rest of your life, cannot be made by one teacher without your parents' permission. Relax, you're not alone in this. Everybody makes mistakes, even teachers."

By the time Joey got home, a murky, dank coldness clung to him. Avoiding his mother, he went to his room and took out the letter from Mrs. Hamlin. As he turned toward his bed, his heart raced. The sheets were different. These were the shark sheets he'd liked in the store. Mama had changed his bed! Frantic, he dived for the bed and lifted the mattress.

"Is this what you're looking for?"

Hearing his mother's voice, Joey jumped. She stood in the doorway, holding the package of cupcakes.

"I told you about keeping food in your room. And in your bed! Joey, you don't even like cupcakes like these," she said. "I took an hour from the beauty shop to buy those shark sheets you wanted so much a few months ago, just to thank you. Joey, you and Franklin working together on Sunday meant a lot to me."

"Thanks for the sheets, Mama. I'm sorry," Joey said.

"Food in the bed leads to mice and roaches." She shook her finger at him. "No more. Promise?"

"I promise, Mama. I'm sorry," Joey said, apologizing for far more than she knew. She handed him the cupcakes. He went downstairs with her and threw them into the garbage can by the door.

During dinner, Joey picked at his food, pushing the asparagus so far to one side that three stalks fell off the plate. He put them back. Joey listened with one ear to Mr. Johnson's talk about the contracting business and the pickup truck. Mama appeared to be too absorbed to notice him. Over in the corner, Josie wore the same woebegone expression that Joey did. He felt like giving her a thumbs-up sign. We're two of a kind, me and Josie, he thought.

"What's wrong, Joey?" asked Mr. Johnson, laying down his fork.

"Nothing." Joey pushed the mound of mashed potatoes to the center of his plate.

"No more 'nothing' answers. Now, you tell us what has you looking that miserable."

Mama and Mr. Johnson turned their attention to him.

"Okay. I have to show you something."

Minutes later Joey returned with the letter from Mrs. Hamlin. The table had been cleared. Mama was pouring two mugs of hot tea. A half-full glass of milk remained at his place.

Mr. Johnson reached out and took the letter. Joey watched him as he read it. Curiosity, concern, and anger crossed his face like flashes of lightning. He pounded the table, shouting, "No! I won't stand for this!"

"Let me see that!" Mama snatched the letter, almost knocking over her mug. Joey's mouth dropped.

"Who does she think she is? This boy has no business being in some special class! I won't let this happen to him!" Mr. Johnson paced up and down the length of the kitchen, ignoring Josie's nervous barks.

"Let's calm down. Tell us what happened," his mother said.

Joey repeated the story while part of him watched Mr. Johnson. He had never acted this way before. In fact, Joey could not recall a time other than during the wedding and at the purchase of the 1953 Chevrolet pickup truck when he'd seen Mr. Johnson show any strong emotion.

"Ernestine. Baby. We have to stop this and do it immediately. Look, I'll go to school with Joey tomorrow morning and straighten it out." Mr. Johnson clenched and unclenched his hands.

"Honey, what's the matter? I've never seen you this upset. I can take care of this. I'm Joey's mother. That teacher can't do anything without my consent," his mother said.

"Labeling a boy because he's upset or displaced or because they won't take the time to teach him and teach him hard—that's worse than wrong. That is criminal, Ernestine. No matter what school I was put in, I saw too many of our boys labeled 'slow,' and stuck in the low reading group all year long, then tracked through school at the bottom." Mr. Johnson sank into his chair. "Too many of them didn't have anyone who knew how to fight the system. I made sure that I learned how to."

"Oh, honey, that was a long time ago. You're the smartest, kindest man I know." Mama handed the letter back to Joey and embraced her husband. Josie jumped up on him.

In a shaky, low voice, Joey heard Mr. Johnson say, "No, sometimes long ago is right now. I spent years with no one to love me or stand up for me. Until Mike and Josie, but that wasn't like a family. Until you and Joey . . ."

"Mr. Johnson, you'd go to school for me?" Joey was stunned by his stepfather's behavior.

Mr. Johnson's head swerved around and his gaze probed Joey like a laser. "I'd like to go to school with you and your mother tomorrow. And we will be meeting with the principal about this. Her name is Mrs. Mack, right?"

Joey nodded.

"Franklin, you don't have to go. I know you want to save

your days off for Thanksgiving and Christmas." Ernestine caressed his cheek.

"Ernestine, I want to go. This is more important than any holiday. We'll go together." Mr. Johnson stood up. "You got homework to do, Joey?"

"Yes."

"Then get to it. Was there anything else bothering you?"

Joey thought about all the things that were on his mind. But this wasn't the time to talk. "Nothing. Thanks. I mean, I'd better get my homework done," Joey stammered, careful not to say "Mr. Johnson."

Sometime during the night, not too long after he'd gone to bed, Joey stirred. Some internal alarm warned him that his bedroom door had opened. Still half asleep, he saw a tall man standing there, staring at him. Mr. Johnson. Joey fell back into sleep.

Thursday morning started off like a tornado. Joey watched as Mama called the school and firmly requested an immediate appointment with Mrs. Mack. Then she went down to the shop. Joey saw a relieved expression on her face when she returned.

"Gladys and Susie said that they will be glad to work on my morning customers. Franklin, you ready? Josie, get over here and eat. Joey, finish your breakfast," she ordered, moving from one end of the kitchen to the other.

Before Joey knew it, they were at school.

The school office seemed to shrink when Mr. Johnson strode in, leading the way. Joey watched the secretary, Mrs. Steller, hurry over to them. They sat for fifteen minutes before she gestured for them to enter the office. Mrs. Mack stood and held out her hand. Joey edged close to his mother as she handed the principal the letter. In silence, Mrs. Mack read the letter.

"I did not know anything about this. Tell me what happened," Mrs. Mack said, taking out a notepad and a pen. "I'm going to take notes. Is that a problem?"

"The only problem we have is with this Mrs. Hamlin. Joey is smart. And he does not have any cognitive or language processing or attention deficits. In fact, he should be tested for gifted class," stated Mr. Johnson in a measured but firm tone, pacing each word. "Serious attention deficits tend to show up much earlier in children. Especially in boys. Joey responds well to directions both orally and in writing. He has powerful concentration abilities, especially in the areas of study that interest him. This is true for many boys, as you know, Mrs. Mack. He does not exhibit attention deficits in any language processing area that his mother and I are aware of."

Mama and Joey stared at him. Joey wondered where Mr. Johnson had learned all those big words. A glance at Mrs. Mack's face told him that she was impressed.

"My, I see that you know this area, Mr. Johnson. Joey tested borderline gifted some years ago. I do agree that it is not the accepted procedure to have a letter like this go home without considerable prior consultation. However, Mrs. Hamlin is a new teacher and may not know the proper procedures to follow before—"

Joey's mother and Mr. Johnson interrupted at the same moment. "That is no excuse!"

Inside, Joey smiled.

"I agree. But Joey's performance has shown some decline. He's had problems in class," continued Mrs. Mack, her voice as professional as her dark gray suit, crisp white blouse, and pearls.

Mama leaned forward. "We know that, Mrs. Mack. Joey is adjusting to some difficult changes in our family. Divorce and remarriage are hard, especially on children."

"He needs guidance and support, not special classes. Not a teacher who singles him out for this kind of treatment," argued Mr. Johnson.

"Are you suggesting that we place Joey in another classroom?" The principal folded her hands. Everyone shifted their attention to him.

Joey thought about D.J. and, unwillingly, about Denise. He did not want to leave his friends. Plus Clark and his gang would think that he was a coward. Doc's words about choosing doors came back to him. This was a time for choosing doors. Another classroom with another teacher would be easier. But did easier equal better?

"I want to stay in Mrs. Hamlin's room," Joey decided.

"All right," murmured his mother.

Mrs. Mack took out a sheet of school stationery and wrote a note. She placed it inside an envelope and sealed it. On the front of the envelope she wrote something.

"Let's dismiss any consideration of special classes for Joey. Joey, give this to Mrs. Hamlin. What else can I do?" she asked. Joey held onto the envelope.

"We'll work our problems out as a family. It's our responsibility, not the school's, not yours or Mrs. Hamlin's," stated Mama.

Mr. Johnson clutched his wife's hand. "But we want you to talk with Joey's teacher." He reached for the letter Joey had brought home. "And please tell her to follow the established procedures before sending us a letter like this. Joey is talented, very talented." With that, he handed the letter back to the principal.

"Mr. and Mrs. Johnson, I will have a conference with Mrs. Hamlin. I appreciate your coming in." Mrs. Mack extended her hand.

Joey stood up, not believing what had happened, not even able to understand what had happened, other than that he would not be tested for a special class. Something had shifted inside the space that he, his mother, and Mr. Johnson shared.

"Oh, Mrs. Mack, my husband and I talked it over last night: We would like to have Joey referred for testing for gifted class as soon as possible. Mrs. Mack, will you help us?" Mama faced the principal again.

"Yes. It may take some time, but I will get the process started. Joey, you are very fortunate to have this kind of love and support. By the way, Mr. Johnson, where did you learn so much about special education?" Mrs. Mack smiled.

"I did a lot of reading. A whole lot of reading," he replied. "And for a few years I tutored delinquent boys."

"I certainly commend you, Mr. Johnson," said Mrs. Mack.

Outside the office, Joey hugged his mother, careful that other children did not see him. Remembering all that Mr. Johnson had done and said, he thrust his hand out. Mr. Johnson grasped it. His hand felt large, strong, and warm.

By the time Joey walked into Mrs. Hamlin's room, the reading groups were writing in their journals. He handed her the envelope. Mrs. Hamlin glared as she read the contents. About a half hour later a messenger came in and Mrs. Hamlin left, informing them that the intercom was on. That meant that the office, including Mrs. Mack, could hear what was going on in the room.

"Where have you been?" whispered D.J.

"Probably in the principal's office," goaded Clark.

"Right for once, Clark. But not for the reason you think," Joey replied.

"What reason? Are you the new janitor?"

"Stop it, Clark," Denise hissed. "You are in worse shape than a starfish."

Joey and D.J. laughed.

"So you let girls speak up for you." Blue eyes like ice chips taunted Joey.

D.J. started to say something, but Joey touched his arm. "Clark, I hope you get lucky, just like the mastodons, mammoths, giant ground sloths, saber-toothed cats, and giant beavers." He rattled off the names.

Both of his friends frowned, clearly puzzled.

Clark tensed visibly. "That's the kind of dumb, stupid thing you'd say," he replied with a shaky laugh.

Joey thought about telling him the punch line. He decided not to, but he couldn't let D.J. and Denise suffer all day. He wrote the word *dinosaur* on a piece of paper so that D.J. saw it. D.J. rocked with laughter. Joey slid it over to Denise. When Joey made a cutting motion across his throat, she joined in.

Clark lunged for the paper. Joey snatched it and thrust it into his jeans pocket. He wondered if Clark would ever realize that all of those animals were extinct. Probably not.

Clark reached across the desk, then turned away with the threat, "I'll get you back, Joey Davis! You just wait! Nobody laughs at me!"

Joey, D.J., and Denise continued to laugh at him, covering their mouths to keep the noise down. Clark glowered and thrust his head into a football magazine. The door was open and Miss Alder looked in every ten minutes to check on them. Joey liked seeing her.

About forty minutes later, the classroom door banged shut. Mrs. Hamlin glared at the class. She caught Joey's eye and her face reddened. Breathing hard, she marched to her desk. The rest of the morning, Joey felt Mrs. Hamlin's hostility aimed at him. What had Mrs. Mack said to her?

After recess, Joey returned to the classroom in line, just behind D.J. Mrs. Hamlin headed the line. As usual she had forgotten to lock the classroom door. When they entered, the children gasped and ran back out. Mrs. Hamlin started hollering, "Who did this? Who did this?"

Shocked, Joey stared at the vandalism. The entire science center was a shambles. The table had been knocked over, with containers opened and bottles smashed. Water, pebbles, and sand were splattered everywhere. Insects crawled all over the room. Whoever had done this had even ripped up the instruction booklet! Quickly, Joey began to collect the insects. Maybe something could be salvaged.

Out of the corner of his eye, Joey saw Clark sidle up to the teacher. "Mrs. Hamlin, I saw Joey leave the yard and come back into the building."

"Me, too," piped up Anthony.

"Is that true, Joey?" Mrs. Hamlin put her hands on her bony hips. "Get over here and explain yourself."

"I came back in to go to the bathroom. I got permission from the yard supervisor. You can check with her." Joey glared at Clark. "You did this to get back at me."

"Prove it," Clark said. "I was in the yard for the whole recess. Right?"

A chorus of voices agreed. Anthony grinned. Even D.J. nodded. Joey gazed around him. "Where were you, Anthony?" he asked.

"I had to go see the nurse."

"You're lying! Check, Mrs. Hamlin. He did it. Clark put him up to it," Joey said, moving closer to the two boys.

"I want this room cleaned up. And, Joey, you have no business accusing anybody of anything," Mrs. Hamlin replied.

"I did not do this." Without another word, Joey took his seat. D.J. and Denise sat next to him, forming a shield.

"I can't prove that you had anything to do with this vandalism, Joey. Maybe Anthony did. But I'll be keeping my eye on you from now on," warned Mrs. Hamlin, pointing her finger at him. "I still believe that you need special help. Now, Alexander and Sharon, select five students and straighten this up."

By the time the day had ended, Joey was exhausted. He talked to himself all the way to his bicycle. "I had the chance to get moved to another room. I'm the one who decided to stay. So I'd better learn to prevail in there with her and Clark. But maybe I *should* have chosen another door."

Separating from D.J., Joey bypassed Doc's and rode home. At least he was going to be tested for gifted. Thanks to Mama and Mr. Johnson, there would be no special class for him. Joey managed to relax as the sunlight warmed the back of his neck. He hoped that Daddy would call tonight. Maybe Daddy wouldn't get the job in Chicago. Maybe. Just maybe.

6

By late Friday evening, Joey's head ached. Not only had there been no word from his father, but he realized that the next morning he had a promise to keep. He could hear Mr. Johnson in the backyard. Joey still couldn't believe the way his stepfather had acted at the meeting with Mrs. Mack. Mr. Johnson was full of surprises. Yet the thought of spending an entire day alone with him was unsettling. Working together on the gutters was not the same as going off in that odd truck with Mr. Johnson. This would be something new.

He watched Mr. Johnson hose down the pickup, wash windows, and polish the forty-year-old chrome until it gleamed. Work lights hung from the doors of the garage. Josie danced about, her tail wagging. Then Mr. Johnson went into the garage and came out with a box. He held stencils up to the driver's side of the truck and counted out spaces. Joey could not see what he was going to paint. Probably F. Johnson, Contractor, and a telephone number, he thought.

On Joey's desk sat a new form Mrs. Hamlin had passed out, requiring a parental sign-off on homework. At least three hours of homework awaited him, more than most of the other children had. Mrs. Hamlin had insisted that he needed the practice. In addition, Joey had been assigned a series of animal reports for the science-center bulletin board. She wanted two each week.

I've got to figure out a way to do the research and enjoy the extra work, Joey thought. His eyes spied a school picture from the previous year. I know! Each animal will stand for somebody. This week I'll do Anthony and Clark. They'll never know, but I will.

Joey reached for a box under the desk. He lifted the top. Inside were dozens of animal pictures that he'd collected over the years. The animal twins of Clark and Anthony were hidden somewhere among them.

"So what is my biologist, entomologist, oceanographer, and paleontologist up to? See, I got them all right." Mama's slouch against the door frame revealed her fatigue. Fridays meant good money in the beauty shop. Money meant hours of hard labor. She rotated her head from one side to the other.

"Mrs. Hamlin is making me do two science reports a week for the science bulletin board." Joey turned around. "She blamed me for tearing the science center apart."

"Joey, we talked about that. What matters is that you and I know that you are innocent. Life has a way of working out. Stop taking everything so personally. So, are you going to use this assignment as an opportunity to learn?" She sat on the bed.

"Sure, Mama. Animals are *my* thing. Nobody can top me." Suddenly Joey envisioned Anthony as a Komodo dragon, the largest lizard in the world, ten feet long and weighing in at three hundred pounds. Komodo dragons were not the nicest animals, eating one another and dragging off dead goats to rip apart and devour. They didn't even have visible lips. That sent him into peals of laughter. Not that lizards have lips, he thought.

"Joey, I haven't heard you laugh like that in months. I'm glad you're feeling better. What's so funny?" Mama asked.

Joey struggled to regain control. Mama wouldn't find his humor amusing. Making fun of people wouldn't win any points in her book. "I started thinking about different animals I could report on. That's all."

His mother watched him closely. "Are you going out with Franklin tomorrow morning? I packed a lunch for the two of you."

Joey went over to the bed and sat down. "Mama, what will we talk about?"

"That's part of getting to know each other. You'll find something to say. Now, about your father. He'll call. Joey, getting a chance at a managerial position is a big win for him, in so many ways. If he gets the job, then we have to be happy for him. And Chicago is less than four hours away by plane."

"I can't be happy, Mama. He's my father. He's not supposed to live thousands of miles away from me. He has a job here. I hope Daddy doesn't get picked," said Joey.

"That is a selfish attitude, Joey," she replied.

"But you used to tell him to be patient and wait," he argued.

Mama got up. "I was wrong, Joey. Your father should have filed that complaint years ago. He didn't because I was afraid that he'd lose his job and there wouldn't be enough money to live on. But he'd worked hard and deserved a chance." For a moment, regret crossed her face.

"Tell him that. Then you two can make up," Joey urged.

"Honey, my marriage with your father is over."

Joey shook his head.

"Joey, his moving doesn't mean he's abandoning you. He loves you. All this 'supposed to' stuff you talk about is wrong.

People love each other the best they can. How people should love and how they do can be as different as . . ." She paused.

"A horse and an ostrich."

She laughed. "Good for you, honey. Keep your sense of humor. I want you to know that Franklin and I are here for you. If you want to talk about anything, let us know."

Later, when Joey climbed into bed, no phone call had come. Josie strolled in, surprising him. Mr. Johnson followed.

"Just wanted to check and see if you were up for going out on the truck tomorrow." As usual, he waited for a response.

Joey met his stepfather's eyes. He had made a promise to his mother. Breaking it would be wrong. "I'm ready to go. Do I need to bring anything special?"

"No. Just yourself, Joey. Sleep well." Mr. Johnson turned to leave. "Oh, you know that talk we had about your friend who got into trouble? How did things turn out?"

"Okay. Okay." Joey remembered the cupcakes. Unable to return his stepfather's gaze, he looked down. Like a mosquito bite, those cupcakes kept itching off and on.

"Glad to hear that. See you in the morning." Mr. Johnson left with Josie, closing the door behind him.

Cool, early-morning fog darkened the bedroom. Joey lay curled and crunched up close to the wall. Three sharp knocks on the door startled him. Joey roused himself and looked out the window at the truck. It was loaded. What would it be like to ride in that huge pickup?

By the time he'd finished breakfast, Ernestine's Palace of Beauty was perking. Mr. Johnson came in the back door, wiping his brow. It was a good thing that he was not much of a talker in the morning. Unless he has something to say, Joey thought. Like at the meeting with Mrs. Mack. He sure talked that morning.

"Ready?" asked Mr. Johnson, making a bacon sandwich and wrapping it in a paper napkin. "Don't tell your mama you saw me do this. You want to get that cooler she packed?"

"Sure," said Joey, placing his utensils in the sink. He grabbed his jacket and lifted the cooler.

Josie barked. Mr. Johnson took the cooler and put it in the back of the truck. Joey circled the truck. All he saw was a heap of junk. The front window had a strip of aluminum running down the center. He'd never seen that before.

Joey jumped up onto the running board on the passenger side, where Mr. Johnson had swung open the door. Just then, Josie bounded up and claimed her place on the front seat. Joey reached up to get in. The front seat was high, one long seat with no dividers. He strapped himself into the seat belt his stepfather had installed.

Fascinated, Joey watched Mr. Johnson start the 1953 truck. He pressed his foot against a large black pedal on the floor, the starter button. Next, he gradually pulled out a gray metal knob on the panel. Then he turned the key in the ignition, and the floor vibrated beneath Joey's feet. Gasoline smells wafted through the air.

The gearshift rod, somewhat like the stick shift in Daddy's sports car, pulsated in rhythm with the windows. Joey felt and heard the metallic motion of the truck. Over his right shoulder the window rattled. Loud pops erupted from under the hood.

"What's that gray knob?" Joey asked.

"That's the choke—helps us get started," Mr. Johnson replied.

Joey thought of the king of dinosaurs, tyrannosaurus. That thirty-nine foot, five-ton meat eater with teeth as long as six inches must have sounded like Mr. Johnson's truck. Joey leaned back in the straight, firm seat and relaxed against the wiry warmth of Josie.

"You ready, Joey?"

"I guess so," he said, feeling Josie's tongue against his cheek. "She licked me! She never did that before!"

Mr. Johnson grinned, a rare sight. "I guess she knows that you are a member of the club. Josie is real smart."

Joey frowned. "What club?"

"The Front Seat Club!" answered his stepfather. "Whoever sits in the front seat of our 1953 Chevrolet pickup truck is initiated into the club."

With that stated, Mr. Johnson pressed down on the big black clutch on the floor and pushed the long gearshift rod forward. The gate was open. Slowly he turned the steering wheel, which was three times as large as the one in a car. The truck moved out. Mr. Johnson hit the brake pedal and the clutch and shifted back into neutral. He pressed down hard on the metal emergency brake and jumped out to lock the gate.

As they drove past the beauty shop, Mama stood in front, waving to them, a radiance in her face.

"We're off!" announced Mr. Johnson over Josie's excited yelps and the powerful engine.

They turned the corner and headed for the freeway. The ride got smoother. Whenever Mr. Johnson shifted gears, Joey heard the acceleration respond with a throaty whoosh-whoosh. From his perch, he could see over the tops of cars. He felt as if he were riding a tyrannosaurus!

The ride was noisy, bumpy, and thrilling. When they stopped for a light before going onto the freeway, Joey was amazed that the truck filled the entire lane. At the same time, he fretted about how the massive machine would handle the speed of the freeway.

"Don't worry. This vehicle drives fine on a freeway. Not like a sports car, but for an old, three-quarter–ton Chevrolet with a granny gear, it's not bad."

"What's a granny gear?" Joey asked.

"You're riding in a truck with a four-speed manual transmission with four gears. The granny gear is the first lower gear. It gives us more towing power. This baby has two first gears to pull very heavy loads," explained Mr. Johnson, expertly shifting and braking, then accelerating as they approached the on ramp to the freeway.

Joey inhaled deeply when he heard the forceful sounds of the pickup truck gathering speed. Josie turned and licked his face again. He hugged her.

As they headed into Montclair, an expensive area in the Oakland hills, Mr. Johnson signaled and pulled off the freeway. "Where are we going, Mr. Johnson?" Joey bit his lip when he saw the pained expression on his stepfather's face. He had not meant to call him that. But he couldn't go on forever calling him nothing. Joey spoke up: "I don't know what to call you."

His stepfather turned and looked at him, waiting.

"I mean, you're not my father or uncle. And nobody says

'stepfather,' " he stumbled on, wishing that Mr. Johnson would say something.

"Sounds like your mama agreeing to marry me has caused you some problems." Mr. Johnson turned into a doughnut shop and parked. "Big ones. I need another cup of coffee. We're running early. You want a doughnut? Some milk?"

Joey nodded, accepting both offers, and stayed in the truck with Josie.

After Mr. Johnson returned, cinnamon, apple, and chocolate smells coming from the bag of doughnuts on the dashboard made Joey's mouth water. Joey took out a bear's claw and propped his milk on the dashboard. He considered what Mr. Johnson had said. Problems. Big problems. He decided to pick up where they'd left off. "Uh, I don't want to make Mama cry or make you look that way. What do you want me to call you?" Joey asked.

"I can't tell you that. You choose. Joey, I call you by your name and not 'Son' because that feels right for me." Mr. Johnson extended his legs and rolled up the side window.

"I can't call you by your first name! It isn't right for a kid to call a grown-up by their first name. I guess I'll have to come up with something," Joey conceded, taking the last bite.

Mr. Johnson glanced at him. "You call me whatever you want until you settle on a name." He held out his hand. "I appreciate what you said. I'll try to keep that expression off my face until you work this out. Deal?"

Grateful, Joey reached around Josie and shook his hand. "Deal. Where are we going? What am I supposed to do?"

While Mr. Johnson talked, Joey listened. The truck

climbed into the hills, up and down narrow roads edged by eucalyptus trees. Finally, they turned into a driveway and inched up a hill. A low redwood home surrounded by lush foliage and flowers stood nestled on top of the hill. Joey saw an older African-American man and woman come out and wave. His stepfather stopped the truck in the driveway by the garage.

I'm going to act right. Make Mama proud of me, Joey resolved, standing on the runner.

"Good morning, Mr. Johnson. As usual you are punctual to the minute," called the bearded man, walking forward. "And you've brought Miss Josie, I hope."

"I certainly have, Mr. Hodges. Good morning, Mrs. Hodges." Mr. Johnson shook their hands.

"And who is this fine-looking young man, Mr. Johnson?" asked the woman, who was dressed in a bright-green jogging suit.

Joey stood beside Josie. The couple looked like Doc and his wife, comfortable together, like old friends.

"This is my assistant, Joseph Davis. He's a good worker," added Mr. Johnson, beckoning Joey closer.

"Your assistant?" said Mr. Hodges.

"My assistant and my wife's son." Mr. Johnson gave Joey a look that asked if that introduction was all right.

Joey gave a tiny nod and shook their hands.

"Are you hungry? Can I offer you some breakfast?" asked Mrs. Hodges.

"No, thank you," said Joey. "We have to get to work. We're on a schedule." Mr. Johnson patted his back. Joey grinned.

The couple laughed. "Mr. Johnson, if you ever get another helper, please send me Joseph," said Mr. Hodges. "We could use a young man like him in our business. Right, Ida? Come on in."

Joey stood to the side and listened while Mr. and Mrs. Hodges and Mr. Johnson went over the plans for the greenhouse window in the kitchen. Josie sat in the backyard by the swimming pool, as directed. Mr. Hodges left to work in his study and Mrs. Hodges headed out for her morning walk. Mr. Johnson went back to the truck. Joey followed. He knew it was all business now. No playing around.

"Joey, I meant it when I told them you were my assistant. You'll have to go through three levels of training. You interested?"

Joey nodded.

"All right. The first level is gofer, like *go for*. You go and get the tools and supplies I need when I ask you to and hand them to me the way I tell you to. Remember how we worked together on the gutters last Saturday?"

Joey nodded.

"No difference today. You'll learn the names of tools, how to handle them, and pay attention to how jobs are performed in a professional way, from start to finish." Mr. Johnson unloaded the back of the truck as he spoke.

"What do you mean by *professional way?*" Joey tossed his jacket into the truck, next to Mr. Johnson's.

"A professional contractor does excellent work on time, offers fair prices, and stands behind his work if something goes wrong. I have more business than I can handle. And I don't advertise. My business comes from word of mouth," he said with pride. "One day, with some luck and bigger jobs, we might have another family business."

Joey had never heard his father talk about physical work

like this as being professional. Daddy wanted to be a manager for an automobile insurance company, to have a job where he wore expensive suits and carried a briefcase. He wanted a job with an important title and responsibilities, in a large company where he was one of the bosses. Both men worked, but in different worlds. He wondered what his father would think about him learning how to be a gofer.

"Will it be hard to get bigger jobs?" asked Joey, thinking about how much Mr. Johnson was working now.

Mr. Johnson stretched. "Let's work while we talk. Getting hefty chunks of large contracts or even middle-sized ones isn't simple."

They walked from the truck to the rear of the house, carrying tools and materials.

"Why?"

"Well, you have to know the people in government and big business who have the power to make the decisions about who gets those money-making subcontracts. Being an African-American man puts me outside most of those powerful groups. But, and this is the truth, I won't let that or anything else stop me. I've got a plan," said Mr. Johnson.

"What's your plan?" Joey asked.

"You honestly want to know?"

"Yes."

"First, I am building a strong base of individual customers by doing quality work. That way I get referrals and get more customers. Maybe some of my customers will lead me to others who have the power to recommend or hire me for the big jobs, like housing developments and other buildings. At the same time, I will continue to increase my skills and improve the equipment I have. Then I'll be ready when the opportunities come. Along the way, your mother and I will talk and decide, together, when will be the right time to quit Hudson Corporation and be my own boss," explained Mr. Johnson.

"Mr. Johnson, does being an African American make everything harder for you?"

"The short answer is yes and the longer answer is yes." He smiled at Joey. "Every time an African-American man goes out into the world as a competitor, whatever he goes after is harder to get. I am sure that for some white people it's rough, too. But for different reasons. For us it's always harder. We wear our color, and too often decisions about us are made based on our color, not our ability."

"But that's wrong. I don't think all white people are mean like that."

"This race thing is not as simple as whites being mean or not. It's about companies, institutions, a country that has misused our people for hundreds of years. Joey, almost all the people who run this country and have the power to make changes are white, but only some of them do everything they can to stop discrimination," replied Mr. Johnson. "Anyway, we can't focus all of our energy on what they do. We have to help one another and be our best. Never forget that your choice is to be a plus or a minus. Your daddy is a plus. I am a plus. Doc, Georgia, Susie, Gladys, the Hodgeses, Mrs. Mack. And of course your mother."

"Am I a plus?" Joey asked.

"You will have to answer that for yourself. Being a proud, determined man is like going into battle every day as the enemy. Your father is like that. You can be, too." He wiped his brow.

"How?" asked Joey.

"You've got to have somebody in your corner and a safe place to go to and rest so that you can get up again. That's why your mother, you, and Josie mean so much to me. You all are my home. And every night when I turn that corner, home looks so good to me. Just like everything else, we'll take this one step at a time," said Mr. Johnson, lifting a ladder out of the back of the truck. "We've got a job to do, gofer."

"What happens after I get good at being a gofer?" Joey asked, taking the smaller tools and supplies that Mr. Johnson handed him and carefully placing them on the concrete.

"I'll tell you when you're ready. Take this box of tools while I carry the lumber in. Now, we always go around back. No tracking through their home."

For the next several hours, Joey darted back and forth. After removing the old, flat window, Mr. Johnson had to install wooden strips around the opening.

After a couple of hours of measuring, checking for accuracy with a long carpenter's level, caulking and more caulking, hammering, and rechecking, Joey watched his stepfather carefully lift the box that contained the new greenhouse window onto a large dolly. Joey helped him roll it to the site.

Joey scrutinized the sketch of the greenhouse window on the box. The window angled out beyond the house. It wasn't flat like other windows. He liked the rectangular pattern of glass held in place by metal strips and the way the window jutted out into the air and let in light on all four sides.

Mr. Johnson had told Joey that people liked the additional

sunlight and sense of space they got from a greenhouse window installed in their kitchen directly over the sink. The sight of plants flowering and blooming gave them pleasure. Joey looked closer at another drawing illustrating how the window appeared from inside the kitchen, looking out. There was a shelf in the middle for plants.

Eventually, they took a half-hour break, sitting on the back of the pickup truck and eating turkey sandwiches, cookies, and fruit. Mama had made a thermos of fresh lemonade. Joey enjoyed the quiet lunch. After the break, they returned to work.

With Mr. Hodges's help, the window was raised into place. Mr. Johnson worked with intense concentration, not satisfied until the window was perfectly set. He stripped away old parts, set, nailed, and caulked the greenhouse window into place. The discarded window lay in the truck, to be recycled.

Only when he was convinced that the new window was secure did they all go into the kitchen. There Joey watched and handed Mr. Johnson whatever he requested as his stepfather attached premeasured and precut white ceramic strips around the top and sides of the new window. He gently laid in a larger strip for the bottom shelf. Then he put the middle shelf into place.

When Joey had finished carting out the debris and tossing it into the back of the truck, Mr. and Mrs. Hodges insisted that everyone drink a toast to the new greenhouse window. Joey sipped grape juice.

"Oh, I forgot the finishing touch," said Mr. Johnson. He returned with a healthy plant in a red ceramic pot.

"Mr. Johnson, now don't tell me you brought this for me," said Mrs. Hodges.

"For your new window." Mr. Johnson handed her the plant.

Joey grinned. The greenhouse window was elegant. It even had a handle in the center that opened the top to let in the fragrance of the star jasmine bushes in the backyard. A shiver of pride ran down Joey's back as he toasted with everyone.

Before they left, Mr. Hodges handed Mr. Johnson a check and shook his hand several times.

"Now, you have my telephone number, Mr. and Mrs. Hodges. If there are any problems, call me. I caulked it heavily, so there shouldn't be any leakage during the winter rains. Remember, call me," said Mr. Johnson, standing tall beside the truck.

"Don't be surprised to hear from us again, Mr. Johnson. We're thinking about adding a few skylights and a new deck. Our friends the Coopers said that the deck you built for them four years ago is just as sound as the day you completed the job. You'll get calls from us and our friends," said Mr. Hodges. "Some with good connections."

"Thanks a lot. I appreciate the business." Josie jumped into the cab, followed by Mr. Johnson. Joey closed the door on his side. They took off.

"We've got another stop. Are you up to it?" Mr. Johnson maneuvered the truck down the hill.

"Sure. Where do we go next?"

"To a family in Richmond. I've got to rehang three of their doors. Then I want to check on a job I just won the bid for.

That's out in Martinez. Fine work back there. I was proud of you." Mr. Johnson kept driving.

As they sped along, Joey thought about how he had spent last Saturday and what Mr. Johnson must have been doing. Inside, deep down in his heart, he liked Mr. Johnson's approval.

By the end of the day, Josie was stretched out over his legs, snoring. Joey yawned. His stepfather's face showed the strain of working two jobs with overtime at one. He hardly had any time off, but he seemed satisfied. Abruptly, Joey yanked his head up. He had not thought about his father all day! What if Daddy had called?

"Want to stop here and get something?" Mr. Johnson asked.

Joey stared. Of all the stores along the Berkeley-Oakland border, Mr. Johnson had parked in front of the corner store where he had stolen the cupcakes! The door was open. The same young man was there. Joey knew he had enough money to go in and pay the man for the cupcakes. How could he do it?

"I'll run in. You want anything?" Joey asked. When Mr. Johnson shook his head, Joey leaped out of the truck. He snatched a package of corn chips and laid them on the counter.

"That's forty-seven cents for the chips." The gum-popping clerk took the money and handed Joey his change.

Joey felt stuck. The money for the cupcakes was in his hand, but he couldn't think of what to do next. He ran out of the store, jumped into the truck, and shut the heavy door, ignoring Mr. Johnson's bewildered look.

Unloading the truck took time. Joey labored with his stepfather. As soon as they were through, he ran inside the house. No message by the telephone. Where was Mama?

"How did the day go?" Mama was walking down the stairs, drying her hair with a towel.

Mr. Johnson came in. They kissed.

"You two have been weighing heavy on my mind this whole livelong day," she said. "Well, you look dirty, smell dirty, and move like you're bone-tired and hungry."

In unison, Joey and his stepfather agreed. After giving a sketchy rundown of the day, Mr. Johnson went upstairs with Josie trailing behind. Mama wrapped the towel more securely around her head. Joey followed her into the kitchen.

"I'm too tired to cook. What do you want to eat? Pizza? Barbecue? Chinese?" she said, putting the teakettle on. "Why not get cleaned up first?"

"Mama, did Daddy call? Is he back?" Joey asked.

Slowly, his mother faced him. Twice she opened her mouth and closed it. Then she turned back to the kettle. Gathering cup, teapot, and tea, she prepared the tea and sank down at the kitchen table. Her eyes fell on the line of marks on the kitchen door.

"Mama?" Joey asked again.

"Your father called earlier today. I know this isn't going to be easy for you. Joey, he got the position in Chicago." She hurried on. "And he's so happy! Over twenty-five other candidates, he won! I wish you could have heard him. It has been years since I heard him call himself a winner."

Joey interrupted, the words cold and measured. "When is he leaving?"

Mama took his hands. "Honey, he flew in this morning

and right back out. The management seminar starts on Monday. But he'll be back in about four weeks to pack everything and move to Chicago. You'll see him then."

"No! No, Mama! How could he move there?" Joey demanded. The growth marks on the kitchen door mocked him. Never again would Daddy measure his height and praise him. Never again would Daddy declare him the fastest-growing boy in the universe. No more lines would be added to the top one and celebrated.

"Honey, your father's going to call you tomorrow. Please, Joey." She tried to hold him, but he twisted out of her embrace.

Joey raced past his mother, past Josie and Mr. Johnson. He had to reach the privacy of his room. He shut the door, panting and wiping his nose on the sleeve of his jacket. Joey could hear his mother talking and the sound of his stepfather's response. Curious, he inched the door open and perched by the top banister. Maybe they would send him to live with his father.

"I'll go up to him. Franklin, you should have seen his face. He looked like his father had slapped him. I hurt for Joey. What should I do?"

"Let him be. Joey has to work this out," Mr. Johnson said. "After all, Ernestine, the boy's father is moving to Chicago. That's not next-door. Give Joey some space."

Joey tiptoed back to his room, easing the door shut. Somehow he had known that his father would get the job and move to Chicago. Ever since the divorce Daddy had been preoccupied with building a new life. I hope it includes me, Joey thought.

Joey turned off the bedroom light and dragged the desk

chair over to the window. Outside the wind stirred, rustling dead leaves. Mr. Johnson had turned on the back-porch light. Joey looked soberly at the 1953 Chevrolet pickup truck. As he watched the truck, he thought about the days of crazy salads, pizzas, ball games, and marks on the kitchen door. The holidays when he had a whole family. The life he used to have with his daddy. Joey lowered his head onto the windowsill and sobbed.

7

"Joey, are you ready yet?" asked Mrs. Hamlin. Her shrill voice barely carried above the Monday-morning din. "You have two reports to give."

Denise leaned over and batted her eyes. "Joey, do you need any help?" The brightly colored beads in her hair click-clicked as she tossed her braids, missing Clark by two inches.

Joey shook his head. Quickly he unclipped the pages of his science report. Fumbling through his backpack, he pulled out a folder of pictures. This was the first science bulletin board he was responsible for. D.J. reached down and handed Joey two science books that had tumbled to the floor. With a nod of thanks, Joey added those to the pile on top of his desk.

He'd spent Sunday in his room, burying his feelings in the pages of his science library and finding animal "twins" for Clark and Anthony. When his mother had called him to the telephone to talk to his father, Joey had refused. Both times. Only Mr. Johnson's counsel to leave him alone had saved him from speaking to his father.

"Hey, Joey, you're going to do great! Relax. Nobody knows more about animals than you do," said D.J. "After school we'll stop by Doc's to celebrate. My treat."

"Can I come?" Denise asked.

"No!" replied both boys together.

"Joey, we're waiting," said the teacher. "Class, I'm counting to ten. One. Two. Three. Four. Five."

While Mrs. Hamlin counted, Clark leaned back in his chair.

Joey recognized the familiar sneer and braced himself for the insult. Sure enough, Clark came through.

"What animals are you going to talk about, Joey? Gorillas, apes, monkeys, and baboons?" said Clark, loudly enough for the other children to hear. Anthony snickered.

Denise and D.J. glared at Clark. Joey gathered his report and stood up. He went over to Clark. "Listen to my report. I picked one of the animals just because he reminds me of you. Your twin brother."

As Joey circulated photos and illustrations from his collection, the class quieted down. Clark was watching so intently that Joey decided to skip the animal that was most like Anthony. That way Clark could figure out who his twin was. Joey started.

"Now, I want to tell you about one animal. I'll save the other one until later. I've passed around pictures of animals that you know about. But I decided to report on unusual animals that people don't know much about. The animal of the week for the science center is the—" Joey stopped. "Sorry, I can't tell you. You have to guess. Then I'll show you a photograph of it."

The class groaned.

Joey held up his hand. "But I'll give you four real clues. One: It's an amphibian. That means it can live on land and in the water, like a frog or a toad—but it's not one of those. Two: It looks like a big earthworm and can grow as long as five feet. Three: It's almost blind and doesn't have any legs. Four: It burrows in damp soil in streams or forests and eats worms and insects."

The class looked more and more disgusted as Joey spoke. D.J. had jotted down the clues and was studying them. After a while he threw up his hands. Clark's face got as red as paint. Joey tapped one foot. Even Mrs. Hamlin was stuck. Classmates yelled out guesses, all of them wrong. Finally, Joey held up a large photograph of his subject.

"Disgusting!" Denise exclaimed. Others echoed her. Joey laughed.

"You give up? Good! First, I'll tell you the name of this unique beauty. The bulletin board will have information about it and other amphibians."

"Tell us! Tell us!"

"The animal is called a caecilian. This is a photo of a purple caecilian." Joey pointed to a very long, purple, worm-like animal with slick-looking skin.

"Double disgusting," D.J. called out.

"Oh, one more scientific fact. Caecilians have smooth slimy skin. To be scientifically accurate, they are covered with mucus. What we call snot. Right, Clark?" Joey said, handing the red-faced boy the picture.

Clark threw it across the table and lunged up. Mrs. Hamlin stomped over and ordered him back to his seat. Joey strutted away. He collected his materials and went to the empty bulletin board.

Remaining close to Clark, Mrs. Hamlin thanked Joey and told him that she thought one report a week would be more than enough. Disappointed, Joey reached for the stapler. That meant he wouldn't get to share the animal most like Anthony until next week. He sneaked a look at Clark. The boy seemed ready to erupt.

By the end of the day, Joey was worn out. Ignoring Clark's angry threats and jabs took effort. And too many nights of troubled sleep and worry had left Joey running on empty.

Mrs. Hamlin had covered the blackboard with homework. Reluctantly, Joey folded a sheet of paper on which the teacher had written his extra homework. Nobody else at his cluster had one, not even Clark.

"You still want to go to Doc's?" Joey asked D.J. "We can check out the costumes for Halloween."

His friend smiled. When D.J. smiled, the lush lashes on his eyes moved like a fan. "You bet. Why don't you ask your mother about spending the weekend at my house? At least Friday or Saturday night. I know you wanted to hang around home, but now that—"

Joey knew what D.J. meant. Now that Daddy had the job and wouldn't be back to pack up for weeks, what was the good of hanging around for a telephone call?

Denise raised her hand. "Mrs. Hamlin, can we have a Halloween party next Friday?" she asked.

The room got quiet.

"This class has a party every day. Why should I let you have a Halloween party? You don't pay attention. You don't obey me. I can't think of one good reason why this class deserves a party." Mrs. Hamlin folded her arms.

In spite of himself, Joey agreed with her. D.J. rolled his eyes. Clark hissed. Denise sighed. Anthony booed. The class moaned.

Mrs. Hamlin ordered them to place their chairs on top of their desks and line up. The sound of metal hitting wood reverberated up and down the aisles. Chairs tumbled. Shrieks and boos added to the confusion. The teacher opened the classroom door.

Joey grabbed his book bag and lined up. D.J. followed behind Clark. Suddenly Joey felt Clark push him. Then

Clark's book bag slammed into Joey's back with a thud. Joey stumbled, falling onto his left knee. The pain of the impact made him cry out.

Mrs. Hamlin ran over. Clark dashed past them, but not before D.J. could block him at the door. As Clark tried to wrestle away, D.J. clung to any part of the boy he could grasp. Most of the class had left. The few remaining kids edged past the boys. Denise shook her head and moved on.

"What did you do now, Joey?" demanded Mrs. Hamlin, helping him to his feet. "Clark and D.J., get over here! Right now! And shut that door!"

Joey limped to his seat, barely able to put weight on his left foot. Clark sauntered by, whispering, "Now who doesn't have any legs? Don't start crying and getting a snotty nose, Mr. Scientist."

D.J. took down his chair and Joey's. "Clark, shut up! You hurt him! Mrs. Hamlin, Joey is innocent. We were standing in line. Clark hit him with his book bag. On purpose."

"No, I didn't!" Clark yelled.

"Who else was standing behind Joey? Who swung around?" countered D.J. "I saw you try to hurt Joey."

"Joey, can you bend that knee?" Mrs. Hamlin looked nervous. "I hope you aren't really injured. How can I explain what happened to—" She twisted her hands in tight circles. "Clark, if you caused this, you are in very serious trouble, believe me. Don't even bother to open your mouth. Joey, how's the knee?"

Joey raised his knee. Grimacing, he lowered the leg to the floor. Mrs. Hamlin watched with D.J. Joey gasped from pain. "It hurts bad, Mrs. Hamlin. I know I can't ride my bike home," he muttered between clenched teeth. Joey held back the tears. There was no way that he'd let Clark see him cry.

Mrs. Hamlin hurried over to the intercom and called the office. The nurse was still there. Ordering Clark to go with them, she and D.J. helped Joey down the stairs. Reluctantly, Clark carried Joey's book bag.

An hour later, Clark had been suspended for five school days. He'd left crying, dragged along by his ex-football-star father. Mrs. Mack completed the forms while Joey's mother questioned her. Mrs. Hamlin kept apologizing. Soon Joey was in a car with his mother, on the way to the hospital. D.J. had gone home, promising to call later.

Fortunately the doctor informed them that it was only a bruised kneecap. The X rays did not show any other damage. He wrapped the kneecap and gave Mama prescriptions for pain and inflammation. Joey refused a crutch, but his mother insisted.

During the drive home, Joey stared out the window as they passed the corner store where he'd stolen the cupcakes. What a day! Calling Clark a caecilian in front of the whole room hadn't been worth this.

Home looked good. Josie pushed against the fence when she saw Joey. Mama settled Joey on the couch in the living room, let the dog in, and prepared a snack for Joey. Anxiously, she puttered around the room.

"Geneva is going to have the softest hair in the world. I left the shop so fast I didn't have time to rinse out the conditioner!" Mama laughed, wrapping a second blanket around Joey. "No moving. I put the telephone answering machine on. The doctor said you have to stay off this knee and give it a chance to heal. I plan to have a long talk with

Mrs. Mack about Mrs. Hamlin and what's going on in that room. That Clark! What a bully!"

Joey frowned, knowing that although most of the fault was Clark's, he hadn't been blameless. His mother rattled on as she filled the ice pack and laid it on his knee. When she left, he twisted around so that he could look out the window. Clouds swept along, pushed by the wind currents blowing in across the bay. Cars and small trucks drove past. Slowly, Joey's head drooped. He slept.

When the front-door buzzer rang, Joey jumped. The ice pack fell to the carpet. The crutch was by the table. Joey leaned over and grabbed it. Little by little he pulled himself around and up. Walking with the crutch felt shaky. With a clumsy kind of hopping, he made it to the door and checked the peephole. D.J.!

"Mama said I could come by and see you. She told me to call first, but . . ." D.J. wheeled his bike in and parked it in the hallway.

"Thanks for stopping Clark. If it wasn't for you, he would have gotten away. You hungry?" Joey asked, leaning on the crutch.

D.J. nodded. "Is a caecilian a purple amphibian?" The two boys laughed. "Hi, Josie! What did the doctor say?"

Joey hobbled back to the couch and let the crutch fall to the floor. An uneaten sandwich and bag of potato chips lay on a tray. D.J. perched on the arm of the sofa and reached for the chips and half of the sandwich.

"Eat the whole thing. I'm not hungry," Joey said, lifting his leg up. He reached back and turned on a lamp. "I got a bruised kneecap. See?" Joey unwrapped the bindings to reveal a swollen, bruised knee. Then he rewrapped it.

"That looks bad." D.J. chomped on the ham sandwich. "Will you be able to come to school tomorrow?"

"No. Not for a while."

"You look kinda off. What's going on? Look, Clark got suspended. Just what he deserves! You'll be fine by Halloween. We can still go trick-or-treating together like always." The gleam in D.J.'s eyes spread across his face.

"But if you hadn't caught Clark, Mrs. Hamlin would have blamed me. I bet *I'd* be suspended," Joey said. "I did set up the whole science report to get him. I should have thought it through first."

"But look what he's been doing! Come on, he called us apes and baboons! Joey, he asked for it. You didn't fight him."

"Yes, I did, with my mind. If there's a next time, I'll be smarter and not end up getting hurt," Joey said.

D.J. reached for the rest of the sandwich.

Television and a little talk took up the next hour. When D.J. left, the living room felt empty. Eventually Joey drifted off again, lulled by the silence, the pain medicine, and Josie's warmth against his feet.

"Joey! Joey!"

At the sound of Mr. Johnson's voice, Joey awakened for the second time. "Here I am," he replied. A small lamp cast a soft glow in the living room. For a moment, he expected to see Daddy's lounge chair across the room. Instead there was a small sofa from Mr. Johnson's house and two brass lamps.

"What happened to you?" Mr. Johnson asked as he examined the leg, gently handling it while Joey spilled out the entire story, even the part about the science report. Nodding, his stepfather got up, left, and returned with a fresh ice pack and two cans of soda.

Perhaps it was Mr. Johnson's steady nodding and bits of smiles. Maybe it was the exhaustion from sleepless nights. Maybe it was Josie's licking his face and D.J.'s standing up for him. Whatever, Joey told Mr. Johnson about everything that was going on in the room and about his still wanting to be in the gifted class.

"I'd put all of that on the back burner and concentrate on healing this knee. You don't need a test to make you believe you're smart and gifted, do you?" he asked.

Joey was at a loss for words. That was a tough question. Slowly, he shook his head from side to side.

"Work on believing that. Now, how does this feel?" asked his stepfather, positioning Joey's leg on top of a pillow. He had rewrapped the elastic bandage and tucked the ice pack around the knee with a towel wrap.

"Better. Thanks." Joey leaned back. Being hurt wasn't all bad. Josie had licked his face. Mr. Johnson had made him more comfortable. D.J. had visited. Mama had fussed over him. Life could be much worse.

Dinner that night was Chinese food and chocolate cake. Afterward Mr. Johnson carried Joey up the stairs. The knee throbbed.

Later, when the telephone rang, Joey knew it was his father. He turned to face the wall, glancing over only when his mother came in to check on him before going to bed. Then Joey clutched the worn stuffed animal, Dog, and closed his eyes.

Tuesday and Wednesday passed. Joey got more and more bored. Cold rain lashed against his bedroom window both days. The furnace kept turning on, sending heat up the stairs and into every corner of the house. Periodically his mother left the beauty shop to peer at his knee and feed him. She was very strict. Joey had to stay off his feet. She only let him visit with D.J.

By Thursday night Joey yearned for school. The only problem was that he couldn't ride his bike yet. Maybe Mama would drive him. He didn't need the crutch. But he knew his mother wouldn't let him return to school until Monday.

Joey couldn't ignore the Friday-morning sunshine. A tray with milk, cereal, and fruit sat on his desk. He could hear Josie barking in the yard. He moved his leg, waiting for the jolt of pain. It came, but was blunted, the sharp edge flattened. Joey limped to the window. The pickup truck didn't look as ugly to him. He knocked on the windowpane, attracting Josie's attention. She stared up and barked a greeting.

My plans for the weekend are ruined. No way Mama will let me stay overnight at D.J.'s. And how can I be a gofer with this knee? Depressed before the day began, Joey sighed.

Over breakfast on Saturday morning, Joey watched Mr. Johnson load the truck for a painting job. Limping only a little, he put on his jacket and opened the kitchen door. Memories of his first Saturday ride in the truck returned. The thought of staying home all day with nothing to do was too much to bear. Summoning his courage, Joey stepped outside.

"Mr. Johnson, uh—"

His stepfather slid the extension ladder into position and closed the back of the truck. Joey walked over, hoping that wearing his jacket signaled his question.

"So, looks like you're walking better, Joey."

"I feel fine. Can I—I—" Joey stuttered, afraid to ask.

"Let's make this easy on both of us. Would you like to go out on the truck with me and Josie?" Mr. Johnson asked, holding back a smile.

"Yes, sir, I would. I can help." He added, "What about Mama?"

Mr. Johnson laughed. "I talked to her last night. It's okay, as long as I don't make you do anything too strenuous, she said."

"My knee feels fine. Thanks." Joey maneuvered his way into the truck, grateful to be out in the world again.

The painting job took most of the morning. Over his stepfather's protests, Joey hauled paint, rollers, cloths, and brushes. Josie lay outside, behind the house. During breaks Joey took her water and food. Later, for lunch, they stopped at a take-out place.

"Here. Fries, chocolate milk shake, and cheeseburger. Josie, keep out of his food!" Mr. Johnson handed Joey napkins and ketchup.

As he ate, Joey gazed out over the rounded hull of the hood. Children with their parents carried bags of food. He saw boys with their fathers. Their own fathers. He sipped the milk shake.

Mr. Johnson seemed lost in his own thoughts. Joey wondered what they were. Does Mr. Johnson want his own son? For him and Mama to have a baby? Then who will want me? Joey swallowed hard. I wonder what Daddy is doing now. I wonder if he misses me as much as I miss him. The next time he calls, I'm going to talk to him.

The afternoon sped by as they stopped at another home

and a business, doing small jobs: putting in windows and estimating a bathroom redecoration. By the end of it, Joey's knee ached. I won't let Mr. Johnson know. If I do, he'll feel bad about letting me go, thought Joey, grimacing as he shifted his left leg to a less painful position. The bumpy, rocking ride aggravated Joey's discomfort. Hiding behind the bulk of Josie's body, he clutched the side of his leg.

"Hurts now."

Joey's eyes widened. Was Mr. Johnson a mind reader? "No, no pain at all, sir."

"Yeah, I know, and I'm a caecilian or one of your other fancy animals! You worked hard today. A few more trips out on the truck and you'll be ready to move up."

"What's the next level?"

"You've earned the right to know, but you're not experienced enough to move up there yet. You will be. Level two is holder. It takes a certain kind of intelligence to hold on to something, like a piece of wood, and keep your hands steady. That means not only holding wood while I cut, nail, or caulk, but much more. Now, when we get home, you hit the bed. I'll unload the truck. Then I'll ice down that knee," he said. "Thanks; we got all the jobs done today."

Joey watched his stepfather unlock and then carefully lock the gate. He limped up the back stairs. Getting to level two, holder, would take more time and work, but he was determined to get there. Before he knew it, he was in bed, fed, with his knee iced and elevated.

On Sunday Joey stayed home while his mother went to church. Mr. Johnson left to work on a job, leaving Josie behind to keep Joey company. Restless, Joey walked out back. His knee felt strong. There stood his bike in the garage.

It seemed like years since he'd jumped on and pedaled off.

I hate not being able to do anything! he thought. The knee feels fine today. I can't stand sitting around here all day by myself. It's been almost a week.

Joey got the bike and went to the gate. Josie sat by the back steps. The thought of moving beyond the gate on his bike was too tempting. Just for a short ride, Joey promised himself. Real short. He unlocked the gate and wheeled his bike through.

Eager to head off, Joey pushed the gate back. When his left leg hit the pedal, he felt a twinge. But the promise of even one hour out on his own was stronger than anything.

Joey sniffed the autumn air. Soon winter storm rains would sweep through the Bay Area. There wouldn't be many more great days like this one. A whole wonderful morning just for himself. No responsibilities. No worries. Eagerly, Joey raced off.

8

As Joey rode, he forgot about his knee. Doc's drugstore was closed on Sundays, so he headed for D.J.'s. Although he rang the buzzer six times, no one answered. That meant everyone was at church. Maybe I should have stayed at home with Josie. Especially since Mr. Johnson was nice enough to leave her there with me. Disappointed, Joey decided to ride around.

Traffic was light, making it easy to dart among the cars. With dexterity, Joey angled his way up and down streets to the park. Pumpkins sat in windows. Witches and goblins decorated stores. Halloween! It was less than one week away. Joey began to feel better.

The heady smell of the eucalyptus trees bordering the paths excited him. Joey threw his head back and cheered. It felt so good to be out in the world, riding. Wildly, he jumped a curb and whizzed down a narrow pass, taking a sudden curve to the right with ease. He whooped with glee. "I'm free! Free! Free!" he yelled to the treetops.

Hours must have passed. When Joey's stomach growled, he realized that he'd been gone far too long. Mama would soon be home from church! The thought of facing her wrath sobered him. Joey pumped as hard as he could, trying to turn back the clock. At last, he saw his street and turned. There was no sign of activity in the house. He wheeled up to the gate. It was open.

Joey's insides twisted with fear. No! I always lock it! I had to lock it! Mama must have left it open.

He dropped the bicycle and searched the yard and garage.

No Josie. Frantic, he raced up the back stairs and unlocked the back door. The kitchen was empty. Joey mounted the hall stairs two at a time. No Josie. The door to his mother's bedroom was ajar. He peeked in. Empty. Down the stairs he ran and outside to the front of the house.

Joey tried to think. Maybe Mr. Johnson had come back and taken Josie with him. Sure, that was it! But if that was true, why was the gate unlocked, swinging freely in the breeze?

He ran around the yard, then took off down the street to search for the dog. An hour later, he sat panting on the front steps. No Josie. She had to be with Mr. Johnson. She just had to be.

"Joey, what are you doing out here? And why is your bicycle lying in the driveway?" His mother's voice did not match her rich mauve suit and elegant hat. Plus her hand was on her hip.

"I went for a ride. I just got back."

"So you disobeyed me. One of the few times I leave you alone, and you disobey me," his mother repeated as she entered the house. "Put that bike up and lock the gate. Then get in here."

Joey wheeled his bike in and turned to lock the gate. Down the street roared the 1953 Chevrolet pickup truck. When the truck drove into the driveway, Joey searched it for Josie. As it moved past the open gate, he continued to look. He ran around the back of the truck. Then to the other side. No Josie. Terrified, he rechecked the front seat. No Josie. The truck stopped, and Mr. Johnson hopped out. Joey rushed to the back of the truck again. Nothing. No Josie. Where was she?

"I wanted to get home early. Thought we might go to the movies and out to dinner," said Mr. Johnson, smiling. "I got a new job, painting a four-bedroom house. The owners want to sell it. The Hodges recommended me. Time to celebrate!"

Joey stood where he was, gulping back the tears.

"Honey! How did everything go?" yelled his mother from the house.

Mr. Johnson shot Joey a frown and went to his wife. Joey stayed where he was. A few minutes later, he heard his stepfather calling, "Josie! Josie! Come here, girl!" Over and over again. Joey felt the pounding of Mr. Johnson's feet down the stairs, through the kitchen, and out the back door. He felt the lighter sound of his mother's high-heeled shoes tapping behind Mr. Johnson. Joey was rooted to the small plot of grass.

"Joey, have you seen Josie? Where is she?" Mr. Johnson ran to the garage and checked the bushes behind it. "Joey, answer me!"

"Answer him, Joey!"

Mr. Johnson shook him. "Where is Josie? Tell me!"

"I—I left—" Joey stopped, choking.

"Oh, Joey!" cried his mother.

"Where is my dog?" thundered Mr. Johnson.

Joey looked into a face flooded with fear and anger. "I left the gate open. I think she got out."

The silence in the yard lasted seconds, the longest seconds Joey had ever lived.

"How long ago?"

Joey thought. "About four hours."

"How could you do this? You mean you took off on your bike and left the gate open? You let Josie get out? How irresponsible can you be?" Mr. Johnson's voice bellowed.

The telephone rang. Mama ran to answer it, saying, "Maybe it's about Josie."

"I don't ask much from you! Hardly anything at all! Do you know what Josie means to me? Do you even care?" screamed Mr. Johnson.

"I'm sorry," Joey mumbled.

"Sorry won't cut it this time. She's family to me. Do you hear me, boy? Family." Mr. Johnson stared at him with such intensity and anger that Joey blanched.

"I care about Josie, too."

His stepfather tossed his head like a wounded bull elephant. "Don't talk to me about who you care about. Caring means being responsible! Were you responsible today? All you thought about is what you wanted! If anything has happened to Josie—" The threat hung in the air between them. Just then Mama came to the doorway and told them it was a wrong number.

Joey watched his stepfather race to the truck and back out. He wanted to join him in the search for Josie, but he knew that Mr. Johnson didn't want him in the front seat of the truck. He was out of the club. Joey collapsed on the stairs, tears cascading down his face. He hadn't hurt this bad since the afternoon Daddy had kissed him and roared away in a car loaded with suitcases. Now he knew that he could hurt that same awful way more than once.

"Get in here, Joey!" called his mother.

Joey got up, wiping his face with the sleeve of his jacket.

His mother sat at the kitchen table, thumbing through a telephone book. The look she threw at him hurt. Mama was beyond mad. There on the counter were Josie's collar and tags. Joey gulped. Without tags, no one would know who Josie belonged to. She would be treated like a stray dog. If Josie wasn't found soon, she could be adopted by a stranger. Or worse, abandoned. The tags were Josie's only real protection out there.

Mama followed his gaze. "Yes, I saw the collar and tags. Franklin forgot to put them on after he groomed her this morning. The chances of losing Josie are a lot bigger than those of getting her back. How could you be so careless?"

Joey stood near the door. "I just—Mama, I thought I closed the gate."

"That dog means the world to Franklin."

"I'd never hurt Josie. I didn't mean to leave the gate unlocked. I was too busy thinking"—Joey heard the next two words resound in his head—"about myself. I was so busy thinking about myself that I forgot to take care of Josie."

Joey cried. "I'm sorry, Mama. I'm sorry."

He recalled all of the times Josie had waited by the front door for Mr. Johnson. The feel of the dog's tongue against his cheek in the 1953 Chevrolet pickup truck mixed with the sights and sounds of the two Saturdays that they were out together. Josie coming to lay her head on him that morning he'd cried on the back steps. Her crouching on the sofa, careful not to jar his knee. And in that moment he learned something.

"I love Josie, Mama."

His mother shook her head. "Sorry and love are just words. They don't mean a thing unless your actions back them up. And, Joey, I haven't seen you do much. Write down these names and phone numbers as I read them off.

We have to check the animal shelters and vet hospitals."

For the next two hours his mother called, and Joey crossed off numbers. The vet hospitals were open only on an emergency basis. And Josie wasn't in any of them. Not in Berkeley, West Oakland, El Cerrito, or Emeryville. Finally his mother slammed down the receiver and held her head in her hands. Joey wanted to reach out and comfort her, but this was all his fault.

All worries about his knee, Clark, Mrs. Hamlin, stolen cupcakes, gifted class, and his father spun away. Finding Josie was the only thing that mattered. Joey leaped up, grabbed his jacket, and rushed out the back door. His mother's demands to come back meant nothing. He ran to his bicycle and out the gate, slamming it, then checking to make sure it was locked. He had to do something.

Down the street he rode, the wheels on his bike spinning wildly. Maybe Josie was near. On a bike he could spot her more easily than Mr. Johnson could in that old truck.

After searching for an hour, Joey swung by D.J.'s. Two working together could cover more ground than one. It took D.J. seconds to get permission from his father to help Joey. He hurried out, his bicycle bumping down the steps.

"How long has she been gone?" D.J. zipped up his jacket.

Joey let out a breath. "Too long. Hours. We called all over, but she isn't at any vet hospitals or pounds."

"You called the ones close by? What if she isn't near?"

"How could that happen?" Joey frowned as they took off.

"I don't know, but it's a possibility. She may just be wandering around. Does she know her way home?" D.J. asked.

"No, I don't think so. She's always in the truck or in the yard. Except when Mr. Johnson takes her for a walk."

"That's bad. She could be anywhere. And with no tags."

The boys searched streets, parks, and passageways until the sun sank into the bay water. When they reached D.J.'s, Joey nodded his thanks. D.J. clasped Joey's hand and made him promise to call him as soon as something happened.

"D.J., do you blame me?" Joey asked.

D.J. halted in midstep and turned around. "You sure messed up. But I don't think you meant to let her out. You're not like that."

Joey gazed off down the street.

D.J.'s expression shifted. He wheeled closer to Joey. "Do you think you did?"

A freezing burst of wind swept down the quiet street. Soft lights shone from the apartment and house windows. Behind the lights, Joey envisioned families eating dinner with their dogs. Real families with good fathers and mothers who never divorced, surrounded by their children. But the vision blurred and evaporated. As hard as Joey tried, he couldn't hold on to it. Real was what was happening right now. Joey probed his mind and heart.

"No, I didn't do it on purpose. Like Mr. Johnson said, what I did is worse than that. I didn't even think about Josie. I was too busy thinking about myself," he replied. "I didn't even check the gate, D.J."

"I've got to get inside. You know how my dad is. Stop blaming yourself. Find her. Call me." D.J. punched Joey on the arm and left.

Joey beat his record home by three minutes. But when he saw the house and the sign ERNESTINE'S PALACE OF BEAUTY, he clutched the hand brakes. What would he find inside? Josie?

Cautiously he sneaked around the back. No Josie. He peeked through the kitchen window. Mr. Johnson and his mother sat at the table, their uneaten dinners before them. His mother was talking to his stepfather and patting his arm. No Josie. That meant one of two things: Either he hadn't found her, or Josie was dead.

Joey parked his bike by the stairs and entered the kitchen. Somehow, sneaking up to his room was cowardly. Anyway, he had to know. Crossing his fingers behind him, Joey stood by the counter.

"Mr. Johnson, did you find her?"

His stepfather whirled around. The dark glint in his eyes flashed.

"Where have you been? You worried your mother to death! No, I didn't find her. She could be anywhere! Anywhere! And it's your fault," said Mr. Johnson, standing up. "If you wanted to hurt me, you couldn't have chosen a better way. I am so angry with you. You don't have to care about me. But what did Josie ever do to you?"

Joey shrank against the counter.

"Franklin, please. We'll find her. I promise. Joey may have been careless, but I can't believe he would do anything like this on purpose," said his mother, rising.

"I can, Ernestine. He's never really wanted us here. Not me, no matter how hard I've tried. Not Josie." Mr. Johnson's implacable stare convinced Joey that his stepfather believed what he said.

"I didn't mean to let Josie out. I love her. I'll find her."

The telephone rang. It was D.J. The boys talked briefly.

Before Joey had walked three steps the phone rang again. It was his father. Joey listened while his father talked on about his success and all of the plans he'd made for the two of them. At the end, as usual, he asked how Joey was doing. Joey told him that everything was fine. There were no problems. He mustered enough enthusiasm to convince his father and hung up.

Not hungry, he fled to his room. Joey stared at the family photograph. Somehow it didn't affect him the way it had before. He walked over to the window. The scarred truck filled the backyard. How could he go to school with Josie out there somewhere?

Sound sleep eluded him all night, so when his mother knocked on the door, he sprang up. He'd gotten up during the early dawn hours, hoping that Josie might be outside. No luck. It took only half an hour to wash up, dress, and pick up his school books. Joey noticed that his knee felt normal.

As he went downstairs, he heard Mr. Johnson on the telephone, telling his supervisor that he would be out that day. Joey knew that his stepfather refused to miss work, even when he was ill. If he's going to spend the day hunting for Josie, then I should, too.

But the expression on his mother's face made him scrap that plan. His stepfather ignored him. Joey snatched a piece of toast and left. In his pocket was a slip of paper covered with the names and addresses of shelters and vet hospitals.

Joey spent an uneasy Monday in school. Life in the room was different. He couldn't put his finger on it, but everybody was quieter. Mrs. Mack came in and sat in the back for half an hour. Then she left.

Mrs. Hamlin made him stay in during both recesses to begin the work he'd missed the previous week. With Clark suspended, the cluster was peaceful. Joey barely heard the chatter about Halloween. He had to find Josie. Halloween didn't matter. While Mrs. Hamlin worked on the other side of the room, Joey took out a piece of clean paper. He began to make a flier. Denise lent him her stapler so he could attach it to trees.

After school he and D.J. headed for a copy store, where Joey paid for thirty copies of the flier. Joey and D.J. drove around their neighborhood, stapling up fliers describing Josie. They questioned every adult and child they saw. No one had seen Josie.

D.J. turned toward home, while Joey took the long ride across town to the animal shelter. He passed the store where he'd taken the cupcakes, but he didn't have time to stop.

The one-story, wooden building was located in an industrial area. Joey noted the list of fourteen shelters posted on the outside wall. He walked in. There was a bulletin board with forms tucked into pockets. Joey saw a woman behind the counter.

"Hi. I lost my dog. She's an eight-year-old Airedale terrier, black and brown. No tags. She's been gone since yesterday morning. Have you seen her?" Joey went through the speech.

The woman checked a book. "No. A man was in earlier this morning with the same description. He filled out a *lost* form."

On the bulletin board, Joey spotted the form left by Mr. Johnson and a small photograph of Josie. There were three times as many *lost* reports as *found* ones. That was disheartening. Joey saw a pamphlet on finding a lost pet. He took one.

An older woman came in with a young woman beside her, holding a pet box. Inside it he heard a cat crying and shrieking. Joey watched.

"Now, Mother, stop wringing your hands. We called. Mrs. Bellini and a cat, Muffin," said the daughter to the volunteer behind the counter.

The older woman clutched her hands together. "I take Muffin everywhere with me. Everywhere."

"Mother, please, she's old and sick. This is best for her."

"Mrs. Bellini, please fill out these two forms. The cost for euthanasia is ten dollars," the volunteer said.

Sighing, Mrs. Bellini completed the forms, handed over a crumpled ten-dollar bill, and without a look at the cat box hurried out, saying, "I can't stay. I just can't."

Joey frowned as the daughter handed over the cat and a man came out and took the box. "Are you positive there's no Airedale terrier back there?" he asked the volunteer.

"Listen, just like I told the man this morning, go back there and take a look."

Joey asked, "If she's hurt, where would she be?"

"I'm beginning to feel like a tape recorder. I'm sorry. We've had so many animals coming in. It's been hard to keep track of them all." She mustered a tired smile.

Joey listened as the volunteer told him that if Josie was found hurt, they would send her to an emergency treatment service center, where she would be stabilized and then brought back there. Reluctantly she added that most damaged animals were killed after five days if they were not claimed.

"But— You mean, Josie could be killed just because she's hurt and lost," he sputtered.

The woman added, "With no tags, she's considered abandoned."

"How do you kill animals?"

"They die by an injection of poison. They go gently with no pain." The telephone rang.

Joey didn't dare ask what was used. "What happens to them after that?" he squeaked out.

"We put the animals in bags in a freezer, and a company comes and picks them up. They are cremated and used for landfill and fertilizer for places like football fields. You want to take a look at the dogs out back?"

Feeling sick, Joey headed toward the open door to his left. Sounds of dogs whimpering and barking tugged him further. Out in the open, he parked his bike by the wall. A long concrete walkway stretched out with numbered cages on both sides. Behind the open cages, he saw secluded rooms where each dog had a full bowl of water and food. The cages were clean.

"Hi, there," whispered Joey as he slowly scrutinized each dog. Their tails wagged. One tan mutt came up and sat down, holding out his paw. He pressed his nose against the locked cage.

Joey knelt down. The dog licked his fingers. When Joey stood up, the little mutt walked back and laid his head on his paws. Joey felt guilty, but he had to leave and find Josie.

On his way out he thanked the woman and grabbed extra pamphlets. "I'll call every day," he told her. "I'll come by every day."

Too upset to go home, Joey stopped by the vet clinic. No Josie. Mr. Johnson had left a photo and form there as well.

There, too, Joey promised to call and come by every day. Then he left to make the long trek across town.

When Joey entered the drugstore he saw Doc at the counter, licking chocolate syrup off a spoon. Without a word, Doc began making another soda. Meanwhile, Joey paced, muttering to himself. Eventually he stopped and told Doc the whole story. Since it was late, Doc called his mother.

"Come on, eat this! I bet you didn't have any dinner last night or breakfast or lunch today," said Doc, laying a plate with a whole-wheat tuna sandwich, pickles, olives, and potato chips next to Joey's soda. "Eat. Then we'll talk some more."

Joey shook his head. "Thanks, Doc. I'm not hungry."

Doc glared at him. "Yes, you are. Eat, Joey. You can't think straight on an empty stomach. And thinking is the only thing that is going to help you."

Convinced, Joey bit into the sandwich. The food tasted great. While Joey crunched on a crisp, cold dill pickle, Doc fixed another sandwich. The second one tasted even better than the first. Joey began to relax.

"Franklin must be feeling very guilty," Doc commented.

"Why? I'm the one who left the gate open!"

Doc scooped up a spoonful of rocky road ice cream. "But he didn't put the collar and tags back on Josie. That makes it impossible to identify her."

"Josie is an orphan," Joey said.

"Worse. She's an orphan without any records," said Doc.

"What else can I do? D.J. and I rode all over today. And Mama called for two hours last night." Joey looked at Doc for suggestions.

"Josie could be just fine, wandering around. Sooner or

later she'll get picked up. Or she could be hurt. Without tags, if she isn't claimed in a few days, who knows. Somebody might intervene and help her. Or she might be . . ." Doc paused.

"Dead," Joey said. "No, I can't believe that. Doc, I know she's alive. We just have to find her. I'll go by the shelters and vet hospitals every day. That's what the pamphlets say to do."

Doc licked the silver spoon. "Good. I would expand the area you're looking at. There's no telling where she might be. I'd call across the bay. If she's injured, somebody probably picked her up. She's that kind of dog, real quality. If we find out who, we find Josie."

Doc pointed to Joey's soda. Obediently, he began sipping it. A late rush of customers entered. Doc went to help them while Joey finished up and washed the glasses, plates, and silverware. He wiped down the counter. Then he got ready to leave. Doc came to lock the door behind him.

"Remember what I told you about choosing the right doors?"

Joey nodded.

"We all make wrong choices. But then we can decide to make up for them by being strong and solid at every opportunity. Opportunities add up." That said, Doc gave Joey a quick hug.

Joey pedaled through the night as sprinkles changed to cold raindrops. He prayed that when he opened the kitchen door, Josie would be home.

9

By the time Joey had unlocked the gate and eased his bike into the neatly organized garage, his knee hurt so badly that he had to hop up the steps. Mama had left a plate for him on the stove.

"Joey! With that rainstorm out there, I've been worried." His mother entered the kitchen, clutching her robe closer.

"Josie?" he asked.

Mama came over and gestured to him to take off his wet clothes. "You look as bushed as Franklin. He's out searching for her. Still no word. He has to go to work tomorrow. I know that is driving him even harder."

"Mama, the fliers I put up are getting soaked. I'll have to put up new ones tomorrow."

Mama nodded.

On Tuesday morning Joey was greeted with icy silence from Mr. Johnson. Joey had rewritten the flier. With money from his savings box, he had enough to go to the copy store and run off fifty copies. Again he grabbed a slice of toast and fled, mumbling good-bye.

In school, every bulletin board except Mrs. Hamlin's had a Halloween theme. "There's not going to be any more yelling in this room. Not by any of you or me," she said in a controlled, no-nonsense voice. "There are going to be some changes. No more counting to ten. No more getting up without permission."

The class listened. Mrs. Hamlin strode around the room, outlining the new rules and schedules. She reorganized the clusters, keeping Joey, D.J., and Denise together, but moving

Clark's desk next to hers. Joey gave D.J. a wide-eyed look. What was going on with her?

D.J. leaned over and whispered, "Mrs. Mack's been coming in every day, especially last week when you were out. I think Mrs. Hamlin decided she'd give teaching another try."

After lunch, Mrs. Hamlin wrote the schedule for each day on the front board, ordering everyone to copy it down and handing out masking tape. Joey taped the schedule to the corner of his desk. He wondered what they would be doing for science four times a week. Mrs. Mack came in and took a seat in the back.

"Now, we'll line up by cluster every time we leave this room. I'll give you your line-up cluster number now. Write it down on your schedule." Joey picked up his pencil. His cluster was number five.

"Starting today, until the end of November, the cluster leaders are . . ." she continued.

Just before the end of the day, Mrs. Hamlin called Joey up to her desk. The room was quiet. Mrs. Mack had left. Outside the rain continued.

"Joey, I've decided to appoint you, on a trial basis, as science-center leader. That means you'll be responsible for keeping the center straight. I want you to continue your animal reports, but I won't have a repeat of your previous behavior. Is that clear?" she asked.

"Yes, Mrs. Hamlin. But why did you change your mind? You thought I messed up the science center."

Mrs. Hamlin managed her first attempt at a smile. "Clark admitted to his father that he made Anthony vandalize the science center." She cleared her throat. "Regardless, I still expect a major improvement in your grades. Tell Denise to come up here."

Minutes later Denise returned to the cluster, announcing that Mrs. Hamlin wanted her to collect and organize all homework. She beamed.

With Mrs. Mack standing outside the door, the class lined up, cluster by cluster, and walked out in order. Even Anthony obeyed. Joey glanced back and saw Mrs. Hamlin talking with the principal. His teacher looked calmer.

"Hey, Joey, what do you wish?" Miss Alder smiled at him.

"I don't have a wish about me," he said, unable to return her smile.

Joey vaulted onto his bike and waved good-bye to D.J. His friend had to get home. The rain was now a steady drizzle. Joey rode to the copy store, ran off the fliers, and put them in his book bag. Recalling the underlined sentences in the pamphlet on finding a lost pet, Joey raced, thinking, I have to visit the shelters and hospitals in person. Every single day. I can't give up.

Time was against him and he knew it. Mr. Johnson had returned to work, leaving his telephone numbers with the shelters. But Joey couldn't wait for a phone call.

I did that with Daddy. He went ahead and took that job in Chicago. Like I told D.J., this is my responsibility. Mine.

He locked his bike to the meter pole in front of the building. Thunder boomed overhead. Startled, Joey stumbled. He wasn't used to hearing thunder or seeing lightning. It was unusual in the Bay Area.

"Hello, there," said a petite woman behind the counter. Today there was no line of unhappy people. The wide room was empty.

"I'm Joey Davis. I was here yesterday looking for a missing eight-year-old female Airedale terrier named Josie. No tags," he said. "Another lady told me she wasn't here. Can I take a look outside at the cages?"

Joey noticed the hesitation on her face.

"Wait a minute. Let me check." She left and came back with another stranger, a young man with thick glasses. "This is Sam. He was on duty off and on yesterday. We might have made a mistake here. I'm sorry, but we've had an overflow of animals, and two of our four volunteers and most of the regular staff have been out with the flu." The pencil in her right hand tapped two, three times. "I guess nobody wants dogs and cats this week."

"Josie? You know something about Josie?" Joey pressed close against the counter.

"An Airedale terrier was brought in by a man on Monday," said Sam. "No tags. Wait. Let me get the card." Sam hurried away, wiping his glasses.

Joey gripped the edge of the counter.

"Here it is. Sorry for this mix-up. Okay. On late Monday afternoon a brown-and-black Airedale terrier, female, about seven years old, was brought in."

"Brought in. By who?"

Sam paused. "Now, that's the good part, because if someone hadn't brought her in, she would have died. She had no tags and was in shock with a broken leg. We sent her for emergency treatment."

Joey yelled, "Where?"

The woman took over and wrote down the address for Joey. He grabbed the piece of paper and took off.

It was a long, arduous ride. By the time Joey braked in

front of a brick building, he was panting. The waiting room was decorated with attractive sketches of animals. A large cork bulletin board hung on a wall beneath a pair of windows. It was covered with photos of animals that had been found and healed.

Impatient, Joey waited for his turn behind a man who was arguing about a bill for 293 dollars. It took almost twenty minutes and a conference with the vet before the man agreed to pay. Joey was ready to tape his mouth.

"You've got Josie here! Can I see her?" hollered Joey, bouncing from foot to foot.

The vet turned around. "Eleanor, I'll take care of this. Now calm down, young man, and tell me what you mean," she said.

The woman in the white jacket listened.

"My name is Joey Davis. I left the gate open and Mr. Johnson's dog, Josie, got out. That was Sunday. We've been searching for her. She's an eight-year-old female Airedale terrier. She doesn't have tags on her. The shelter said she had a broken leg and was brought here. Please! Please, can I see her?" He was close to tears. "Is she hurt bad?"

"Hello, Joey Davis. I'm Dr. Ingram." She held out her hand. Joey shook it.

"I saw your dog. Do you have proof of registration?"

Joey unfolded a piece of paper and showed her the tags. Mr. Johnson had left them by the telephone, in the kitchen.

"The man who brought her to the shelter came by here this morning and got her. He paid her bills. I didn't get to do the surgery she needs. He was quite taken with the dog and insisted on carrying her to his veterinarian," the doctor explained.

"But Josie's not his! Who is he and where did he take her?" Joey asked, his voice growing louder.

"I have his name and address right here. He lives in Marin County. But I don't know where he took your dog. The hospital, I mean."

Joey copied down the information and got permission to use the telephone. There was no answer. Mr. Kelligan wasn't at home. A glance at the clock told him that there was enough time. He dug into his pocket and found plenty of change. Throwing back a thank-you, he ran outside.

On the corner he located a telephone booth. Mr. Kelligan lived in Sausalito. Across the bay, just as Doc and D.J. had predicted. When he reached the phone booth, only one telephone directory was there. The wrong one.

Joey dashed back to the vet's office. Gratefully, he copied down the names and telephone numbers of all the veterinary hospitals in Marin County. With Dr. Ingram's help, he put marks by the most likely ones.

Back in the cold, wet telephone booth, Joey punched in numbers. Three phone calls later he tried again. Slowly he explained what he wanted to know. He was placed on hold. Numb and tired, he waited, stomping his feet up and down.

A man began talking. Joey listened and retold his story.

"I see. Yes, we are treating an older, female Airedale terrier who matches your description. She's a wonderful dog. Given all the pain she's in, we've had no problems with her. By the way, I'm Dr. Sullivan. Are you the registered owner?" asked the veterinarian.

Joey thought. In a way Josie belonged to him. But he knew who the real owner was. "No, the owner is my stepfather,

Franklin Johnson." He hurried to add, "We have registration and tag proof. Is Josie going to be all right?"

"Tags belong on the dog. Not with you. She would have gotten full care a lot sooner if her tags had been where they belonged." The doctor sounded upset. "Eventually Josie will be fine. I prefer to talk to her owner about the injury," Dr. Sullivan said.

"All right. Look, can we come and get her? When do you close?"

"I suggest you call the man who brought her in for surgery, Tom Kelligan. Of course you can come and get her. But Mr. Kelligan must know about this. He's paying the bills. Can you talk to your stepfather and have him contact me?"

"Sure. Thanks. Please take good care of Josie."

Dr. Sullivan's stern voice carried across the bay: "That's my job."

When the next several coins chimed in, Joey prayed that Mr. Johnson was home. The answering machine came on. He hung up. Without missing a step, he ran to his bike and sped through the rainy darkness. He felt wonderful. He knew where Josie was! And she was alive!

Lights glowed in the living room windows. Mama had closed the beauty shop. Joey unlocked the gate to face an empty lot. Where was Mr. Johnson? Swiftly, he locked the bike in the garage and pounded up the stairs, his book bag swinging beside him. He slipped his shoes off. Mama hated it when he dirtied her floors.

Smiling, he sniffed her meat loaf. Unpeeled potatoes sat on the counter. String beans lay in a pan of water. The lemon cake in the center of the table was sprinkled with white powdered sugar. Joey knew what his mother was doing:

trying to encourage Mr. Johnson to eat. Trying to piece together a family with good food.

"Is that you, Joey?" called his mother.

"Yes, Mama."

His mother sat on the couch. Long white knitting needles clicked, transforming vibrant red wool yarn into a winter sweater for him. Every year she made him a new one. The wan smile on his mother's face wavered. Worry. Fear. Joey ran over.

"I have been going crazy! Calling school and Franklin, trying to find you. Do you know how dangerous it is out there? And I don't mean the weather."

"Mama, I'm sorry. I found Josie! I know where she is. Is Mr. Johnson coming home soon? He has to call Dr. Sullivan right away!"

The back of the raglan sweater slipped to the carpet. Mama stood up.

"Where is she? Why a doctor?"

As quickly as possible, Joey told the story. Mama listened, reading the information Joey had written down. Relieved, she sank back onto the sofa, her hands trembling. Joey sat next to her. He heard the rain pour from the gutters.

"So you were out searching for Franklin's dog. I'm proud of you. A little mad, but still proud," Mama said, adding a squeeze.

The sound of the kitchen door slamming against a wall startled them both. Mr. Johnson was home. Mama rose. Joey's stomach lurched. Since Sunday night his stepfather had ignored him, acting as if he didn't exist. What would he do when he found out that Josie had a broken leg?

Joey shrank against the sofa pillows as Mr. Johnson walked

in. Gathering his courage, Joey stood up to meet him. This wasn't the time to hide. "Mr. Johnson, I know where Josie is." With his mother's help, he repeated the story.

His stepfather looked at him squarely for the first time in two days. "*You* found her? Where's the information? I want to call this Dr. Sullivan and then Mr. Kelligan right now."

The second telephone conversation lasted for some time. Joey peeled potatoes at the kitchen sink while his mother set the table. It was obvious that Mr. Kelligan was reluctant to give Josie up. Only when Mr. Johnson stated that he had the registration papers and the dog tags did the other man begin to relent.

Joey listened. Josie had won Mr. Kelligan's heart in only a few days. But she belonged to Mr. Johnson. She loved Mr. Johnson. He wiped at the quick splash of tears on his cheeks, surprised that he wished Josie loved him as well. As soon as Mr. Johnson had hung up, Joey eased out of the kitchen and called D.J. to tell him the good news.

Over dinner, Mr. Johnson shared what he had learned. Josie had been a hit-and-run victim near the University of California at Berkeley. A girl driving a light-blue car had hit her and sped on. This had occurred on Monday. No one had stopped.

Mr. Kelligan was a professor at the university and had been on his way home. He had spotted Josie lying on the side of the street, moaning. Then a child had told him about the accident. Mr. Kelligan had parked and taken Josie to the animal shelter. Then he'd returned to claim her from the emergency service center and had taken her to his vet in San Rafael. That was where she was now, recuperating from surgery.

"He says that Josie came through the operation well. They

had to put steel pins in her leg to help the bone heal. He just saw her. The hospital is closed now. But I'll go over there first thing in the morning." Mr. Johnson speared a hunk of meat loaf.

"Franklin, I told you Joey wanted to find her. And he did. He kept his word. Our Josie is a tough girl," said Mama, her eyes sparkling.

Joey chewed on a green bean. More than anything he wanted to go with his stepfather in the morning. He had to. When the telephone rang, he got up. It was D.J. They talked for a few minutes. Joey thanked D.J. for his help.

Then Joey returned to the table. "Mr. Johnson, can I go with you to get Josie?"

"You can come." Mr. Johnson began eating again.

"Thanks. I'll be ready. The vet opens at 8:00 A.M. I'll be in the truck," said Joey.

"I'll call your school and explain," said Mama.

His stepfather and mother had their after-dinner coffee and lemon cake in the living room by the fire. Joey cleaned up the kitchen. He cut a slab of cake, poured a big glass of milk, and stole upstairs to his room. He had pages of homework to do. And Josie to face in the morning. Trying to get into the gifted class seemed less important. Seeing Josie was what mattered.

Wednesday dawned clear and bright. Only the ticking of the kitchen clock interrupted the silence between Joey and his stepfather. Mr. Johnson ate his breakfast while Joey eyed the clock. They were to be at the veterinary hospital by 8:00 A.M. Joey dared a quick glance at Mr. Johnson. The skin stretched across his face, drawn and gray. There were dark blotches under his puffy eyes.

The 1953 Chevrolet pickup truck groaned and bellowed as Mr. Johnson warmed the engine. Mama waved from the window of the beauty shop. Riding against traffic, they made good time to the Carquinez Bridge, which linked the northern section of the bay to Marin County.

High above the hood of the truck, Joey could see out over the churning waters. The bridge spanned the water like a metal ribbon flung from one shore to the other. As they sped past the infamous San Quentin Prison, Joey searched for signs of convicts.

"Read the turnoff for me," Mr. Johnson asked, his eyes never leaving the road.

Joey obeyed, and within ten minutes they had parked in front of the hospital. When they entered the building, Franklin took out the registration form and tags.

A short, balding man in a flannel shirt stood by the counter. "Hello, Mr. Johnson. I'm Tom Kelligan." He held out his hand. Mr. Johnson shook it. The two men sat down.

"I appreciate all you've done for Josie. She means a lot to me."

The man nodded. "I can believe that. She stole my heart right away. In a way I'm sorry you turned up." The man stared down for a minute.

"About the hospital fees—the bills, I mean," said Mr. Johnson, standing up. "Whatever the cost, I'll take care of it. And anything else you paid out. That's the least I can do."

Mr. Kelligan started to speak, but Mr. Johnson held up his hand. "Look, I know. Money is only part of all of this. I want you to know you saved my first love. Thank you."

The men smiled at each other.

Soon Dr. Sullivan came out and led them into the rear of the hospital, to a row of large cages. Josie was in one.

At the sight of the injured animal, Joey gasped. Even Mr. Johnson groaned. "Oh, my girl. Josie." The dog hobbled up and, despite the pain, thrust her head through the bars. With each movement she cried. Tears fell down Joey's face. Josie looked so torn up, as if somebody had stomped all over her. And that leg.

Mr. Johnson eased past the doctor and slowly moved toward her. He knelt down, held her head, and murmured to her. Josie's tail wagged. They stayed there like that for some time. The doctor left with Mr. Kelligan.

Josie's right leg was encased in a large support bandage with an open space over the place where the broken bone had pierced her skin. Dr. Sullivan had told them that the open space helped him check for early signs of infection. Every time Josie put weight on the leg, she whimpered. On her side Joey saw places where the impact and fall had damaged fur and skin, leaving raw, red scrapes behind. Joey edged closer.

Soon Dr. Sullivan returned. "Mr. Johnson, Josie needs as much peace and quiet as possible. I can't give her too much painkiller because I don't want her putting weight on that leg. It was a bad break. I put two steel pins in. We'll pull them out in several months. Why don't you leave now? We'll settle her down." Dr. Sullivan gestured to a young woman, who came over, opened the cage, and restrained Josie, not letting her jump up and hobble after Mr. Johnson.

Joey managed to pat her head. He kissed her and held her face in his hand. Josie licked his hand and wagged her tail. How can you look at me like this? I'm the one who got you hurt, he thought. Joey left, wiping at the tears.

Quietly, Mr. Johnson wrote a check to Mr. Kelligan and thanked him again. He met with the doctor while Joey waited outside in the truck.

Joey rolled up the window. Dark clouds were gathering. Before him was the hospital. Somewhere in there, Josie lay in pain.

"Well, I can come and take Josie home in about three days. Dr. Sullivan wants to keep her stable and make sure no infection sets in. He seems to like her," reported Mr. Johnson, slamming the heavy door shut.

Joey nodded, not trusting his voice.

"Since I'm over here I might as well stop at a good paint place I know and get some bids on materials I need. I'll have you back in time for school this afternoon."

Joey risked a question. "Will Josie walk okay?"

"In time, but she's going to need a lot of care and rest."

"Mr. Johnson, I'm sorry. Really . . ." Joey choked up..

"I'm still too angry to talk about this. Seeing Josie like that and knowing how it happened . . . But I can say that your finding her so fast showed real determination and responsibility." With that, he thrust the gear into reverse and backed out.

"But the bills. Will they be a lot of money?"

"Yes, over eight hundred dollars. But the important thing is that Josie's alive." Mr. Johnson shook his head. "Thank God, she's alive."

They got to Joey's school by lunchtime. D.J. and Denise cheered Joey when they saw him. The afternoon was quiet. After school, D.J.'s mother picked him up to go shopping.

With a plan in mind, Joey biked to the drugstore. The store was jammed. Doc dashed from counter to cash register and back. Joey watched. Doc waved to him. Quickly Joey tossed his jacket and parked his bike in the back room.

He hurried to the front and relieved Doc at the cash register, ignoring the surprise of some of the customers when they saw him handling money. When the line ended, he stopped and headed for the soda fountain.

"Doc, I need a job. I'm good at the cash register and anything else you need me to do. And I'm dependable. I won't be late and I'll work on the weekends and after school. Can I?" said Joey in one breath.

Doc squinted his eyes. "Why?"

Quickly he told Doc about Josie and the bills.

"Doc, the least I can do is help pay the cost. Doc, you should see her. Her leg is all messed up. She cries every time she tries to walk. And it's my fault! I did this to Josie! I have to make up in some way. Please, Doc. I'll be a good worker," pleaded Joey.

"So you want me to give you a part-time job working here. Have you cleared this with your mother? Does Franklin agree that you should help with Josie's hospital costs? What about going out on the truck and helping your stepfather on Saturdays?" Doc waited.

Joey swallowed. "I can get Mama to agree. My grades are getting better. And Mr. Johnson wants me to be more responsible. This is a way to do that. Plus he doesn't want me around, especially on Saturdays on the truck."

"Ask them first. Then you and I will discuss your possible hiring. I trust you. I have faith that you can grow past this mess." Doc went back to the storeroom, leaving Joey alone.

Dinner was delayed that evening. Around the kitchen table, no one said much. Joey saw the strain and exhaustion on the faces of his mother and stepfather.

This is definitely not the right time to bring up working for Doc, Joey thought. I hope tomorrow will be better.

10

Thursday morning, drizzle misted the air. Outside the classroom, Joey lined up behind D.J. Mrs. Hamlin marched up and down the line of children, looking more like a marine drill sergeant than a fifth-grade teacher. Once seated, Joey noted that she did not have to count to ten. The room was quiet. Everyone, including Clark, obeyed the schedule and their cluster leader's instructions. Mrs. Mack entered, spoke quietly to Mrs. Hamlin, shot Clark and Anthony a stern look, and left.

Denise worked on a get-well card for Josie. "Joey, I want you to give this to her," she said.

"Thanks."

Later Joey added to the file of activity cards in the science center as the rest of the class prepared to take notes on a nature video that the teacher was showing. He worked quickly. Clark had returned, but somehow that had not bothered Joey. As the video began, Joey reached his seat.

It was a video about animal families. Joey listened as the narrator explained how gibbons paired for life. Examples of foxes, wolves, and beavers followed. Most birds remained together. Beautiful pictures of doves, swans, and finches taking care of their young filled the screen. Joey remembered the crane story.

Just then the video machine broke down. Mrs. Hamlin had D.J. turn on the lights. Instead of getting upset, she directed each cluster leader to collect the notes and hand them to Denise.

"Joey, do you have a report you could offer? We have time," she said.

He nodded, knowing that there were two reports in his book bag. One was for her and one was for Anthony. But giving the hagfish report felt wrong. The jawless, ugly creature had reminded him of Mrs. Hamlin not that long ago. But so much had happened. And it was hard to forget how much trouble his report on the caecilian had caused. So Joey reached for the other folder, grinning to himself. Anthony would never recognize himself as the Komodo dragon.

Struggling to stay composed and serious, Joey began. "The Komodo dragon can weigh three hundred pounds and grow as long as ten feet. I brought a tape measure to show you the length. I couldn't find anything big enough to demonstrate the weight, so use your imaginations. It's too bad that this animal is endangered. On this map you can see Indonesia, the home of the Komodo."

When he finished, it was time for recess. He dared a glance at Anthony. His classmate appeared unaware that the report had been meant for him. Joey laughed.

The afternoon proceeded smoothly. Mrs. Mack dropped in for a few minutes and gave Mrs. Hamlin a brief smile. As his cluster lined up to leave, Denise handed him the card she had made.

"Joey, come here."

"Yes, Mrs. Hamlin."

"Mrs. Mack has arranged for you to be tested for the gifted class next week. Here is the information. If your parents have any further concerns, have them contact her." The teacher thrust the papers at him.

Shocked, Joey took them. Why didn't he feel more excited and happy? Maybe there are more important things than getting into gifted just to show I can do it. Like making Mr. Johnson trust me again, he thought. Joey shook his head. He was surprised to realize how much his stepfather's respect meant to him.

Outside D.J. congratulated him on giving such a solid report and, most of all, on finding Josie.

"But you should have seen her, D.J.," said Joey. "She was in such awful pain."

D.J. sighed. "Yeah, you messed up and it ended up getting Josie hurt. But that girl who hit her and left was wrong. And your stepfather forgot about putting the tags back on after he bathed Josie, so that made it even worse. But you found her!"

Denise echoed, "That's right. D.J., you always know what to say."

Seeing the stunned frown on D.J.'s face as Denise ran off tickled Joey. He watched D.J. get into the car with his mother and two of his sisters, heading for the dentist.

For a long time Joey stood on the school corner, staring at the street. He wanted to ride over to the hospital and see Josie. But that was impossible. His brain whirled. There seemed to be so much that he couldn't do more about, like Josie's being in pain and Daddy's moving to Chicago, but—A thought darted into Joey's mind. Those cupcakes—he could do something about them!

Seconds later, having determined that he had enough money, Joey sped off. When he braked to an abrupt stop in front of the store, he went inside. It took more than physical strength to push open the door. The same young man sat there, perched on a tall stool, popping pink bubble gum.

"Hey, kid. What do you want?"

What could he say? "Where are the cupcakes?"

"Back in the middle of aisle two."

Sure enough, there they were. "How much are they with tax? The chocolate ones."

"Seventy-eight cents."

Joey felt the two dollar bills in his pocket. "Thanks." He picked up a package of cupcakes.

"Here, I want to buy two of these." Joey slapped two dollars in front of the young man.

"Where's the other one?" The gum blowing stopped.

Joey's insides shivered and goose bumps popped out on his arms. "I took it a few weeks ago. Without paying you. I didn't mean to. I never took anything before and I never will again. I promise."

The young man got up and his brown, lanky hair dropped over one side of his face, momentarily covering his other eye. "Let me get this right, kid. Did your parents put you up to this?"

"No! They don't know anything!"

The clerk frowned. "You mean you're telling me this on your own? Don't you know I could call the police? Or your folks? Or the owner?"

Joey nodded. "Will you take the two dollars for two packages of cupcakes?"

The clerk hesitated. They both looked at the black telephone on the wall. Another customer walked in, an older woman. She smiled at them.

"You're the first kid who ever did anything like this. Blows my mind. You got a lot of guts, kid. Okay, pay for both and we'll call it even. Here's your change," said the clerk.

Relieved, Joey jammed the coins into his pocket and held out his hand. The clerk shook it.

"My name's Joey. Joey Davis."

"Okay, Joey. Alan Grant. Now, no more stealing. You got me?"

"You bet. Thanks. Thanks for believing me."

Alan laughed. "How could anybody walk in here and lie about something like that? Go on, Joey. Oh, here." He peeled off a red Life Saver.

Gratefully, Joey took it. On the ride home he let out a loud scream. "I did it! I did it!"

Once home, Joey dialed the animal hospital. Dr. Sullivan was not able to come to the telephone, but the receptionist reported that Josie was running a fever.

"We've got her on antibiotics. She's resting. Don't worry." She hung up.

Joey ran to the beauty shop.

"Mama! Mama! We've got to go see Josie! She's sick. The lady says she's running a fever," he said, skirting around customers, barely seeing Gladys, Susie, or Georgia.

Mama fanned the hot curling iron in the air. "Debra, this cut looks so good on you. I'm going to clip the front a little more and then curl it so it falls to the side. What do you think?"

The young woman put on red eyeglasses and scrutinized her image in the large, oval mirror. "You know I trust you. I like the look."

Using scissors and a black comb, Mama clipped the hair

in small, precise movements. At the same time, she turned toward Joey. "Franklin called me earlier. I know. The vet says that this is to be expected given the state of shock Josie was in. Franklin is taking off from work early and driving over. But I need you to rake those leaves in the front yard and sweep the walk," she said.

"But, Mama, I want to see Josie! Is he going to stop by here first?"

"I don't think so. Get the yard cleaned up. Do your homework and set the table. Check with me when you're done."

A few hours later, Joey's work was finished. He waited on the front steps, watching for the 1953 Chevrolet pickup truck. Twice the telephone rang, first a wrong number and then his father.

"Daddy! How are you doing? You coming home soon?" Joey asked.

The static across the line crackled. "Fine. I love my job. And I found a condominium in the downtown area. Just one bedroom, but there's plenty of room for you when you come to visit, Son. So tell me, what's new?"

Joey leaned against the wall. His father sounded jubilant. And so far away. He wanted to tell Daddy about finding Josie. But how could he make him understand how important it was? So he just chatted for a while and hung up.

Back outside the chilly air gusted around him. Forgetting about time, Joey watched the violet sky absorb the pink streaks across the horizon. The beauty shop closed, but Joey stayed on the porch. By the time the truck clunked into the driveway, it was dark. Joey unlocked the gate and ran after the truck.

Mr. Johnson climbed out. He swung his jacket over his

shoulder and relocked the gate. Without a word he walked around the truck and toward the house. Head bowed, he opened the back door and entered the brightly lit kitchen.

A pot of beef stew simmered on the stove. Mama was mixing a batch of cornmeal muffins. Mr. Johnson hadn't even said hello. Not even hello. I have to ask tonight about working for Doc, Joey thought.

"Honey, what's wrong? Is it Josie? Here, sit down."

Mr. Johnson responded with a wan smile. "Hi, baby. I've got to go back to work tonight. I've taken too much time off. And we need the money. Plus Josie's sick. Sullivan says she's responding to the antibiotics, but that it will take time. That means more bills." He sank his head into his hands.

"Can I go see her when you go next time?" asked Joey, standing near the door.

"Joey, why? Josie can't walk without crying. She's weak from the fever and infection. Every time she sees me she struggles to get near me. Why do you want to see her, Joey?"

If only his voice had been loud, harsh, and condemning, Joey could have withstood the guilt. But Mr. Johnson's voice was anguished, not angry.

Mama threw up her hands. "When are we ever going to start working on becoming a family? That's what I want to know. I realize that Josie is hurt. But she's going to be fine, Franklin. Can't we make some peace?"

"Ernestine, I'm doing the best I can with this. What more do you want?" replied Mr. Johnson, his face set like stone.

"I want a family! What will it take for the two of you to work this out?" Mama tossed the wooden spoon into the sink.

Joey escaped to his room, locking the door behind him. Instead of turning on the light, he sat by the window. Tonight the truck looked big and safe, not ugly. He hadn't even told them about the test forms for gifted class.

Mama knocked, then came in and turned on the desk lamp. "Talk to me." She sat down on the bed, drawing her sweater around her.

"Mama, Doc says I can work for him after school and part of Saturdays if you say yes. My homework is all done and my grades are up. Please, Mama. And I have to give you this. I'm supposed to be tested for gifted this week."

She grinned. "Wonderful, Joey! Mrs. Mack kept her word. I know you're happy about this."

Joey thought. No, he really wasn't as happy as he had thought he would be. "Mama, can I please work for Doc? Just try it out for a few weeks and see how it goes. I know I can keep my grades up. I swear."

His mother shook her head. "That is too much to take on. You get an allowance for helping at home."

"I want to have a real job, Mama. Doc needs me to help out. I know how to run the cash register and stock shelves."

"Is this for the money?" Mama asked.

Mr. Johnson's large frame filled the doorway. Joey realized that he'd been there for most of the conversation.

"In a way. I have to help pay back the vet bills for Josie, no matter how long it takes, Mama. And I like working with Doc. It's different there." Joey mumbled the last part.

"What about going out with Franklin on the truck on Saturdays?"

Joey looked over at Mr. Johnson. His stepfather's face was expressionless.

"Mama, I really want to do this. Please." Joey didn't want to say what he knew, that Mr. Johnson never wanted him on the truck again.

"Let him try it, Ernestine. But only for a few afternoons and Saturdays. If he wants to help out with Josie's bills, he should. Glad that principal kept her word about getting you tested for gifted. At least you have a chance now." With that said, Mr. Johnson left.

Mutely, Joey's mother took the forms, signed them, and gave him her permission to work, kissing the top of his head. "What about Halloween?"

"Not for me, this year. Oh, Mama, Denise made this." Joey got up and handed her the card.

She flipped it open and grinned. "Give her our thanks."

Friday wasn't a crazy day. Peace reigned in the classroom. Joey knew that Mrs. Hamlin would keep her word. There was no Halloween party. Some students brought costumes. Clark wore his father's old football uniform in the school Halloween parade. Denise pranced around the playground area dressed as a princess, complete with a crown.

On Saturday Mr. Johnson took off without Joey. Josie's fever had subsided and she would be coming home that Halloween afternoon. Joey labored in the drugstore, stopping only for a brief break and a call to the hospital. Josie was doing better. D.J. came by and pitched in, just for a Feel Better soda, he explained. They laughed.

From the drugstore, Joey called the hospital again. Mr. Johnson had driven off with his dog. Joey went to work with a will. Finally the shelves were stocked, the floors swept, and Doc's face told Joey that he had done a good job. When

Doc handed him an envelope with his pay, Joey's chest swelled.

"You earned this money. Clean money, the best there is. Dirty money, drug money, buys you two things: jail and death. Remember that, Joey," Doc said, winding the cuckoo clock behind him. "Clean money comes from honest work."

"Thanks, Doc. I'll be here on Monday. Mama said I can work two afternoons a week and some Saturdays."

Tired but exhilarated, Joey stuffed the envelope into his socks and pulled his jeans down. He left quickly. He hopped onto his bike and bent his head against the onslaught of a sudden rainstorm. His yellow slicker was at home.

Joey was about halfway home when he heard a loud horn blasting behind him. The old pickup truck lumbered down the street with Mr. Johnson at the wheel. Joey braked.

"Put your bike in the back and get in here," his stepfather hollered, pulling the truck over and parking it. He jumped out and helped Joey lift the bike into the truck bed under the tarpaulin.

"Why didn't you call? Susie is out sick and your mama had to take over her customers. I'm going to stop and get some pizza before we head home. Here's your slicker and a dry sweatshirt. Take that wet one off. Dry off with this towel." Mr. Johnson turned his attention to the flooded streets.

Shocked, Joey complied. Mr. Johnson was talking to him like a parent! He wanted to give him the envelope, but the time didn't feel right.

"I didn't think about calling." Joey swallowed. "How's Josie?"

"Better. I just dropped her home."

Smelling pizza all the way home made Joey's stomach growl. Mr. Johnson grabbed the pizza and jumped out. Joey wheeled his bike into the garage and locked the gate.

Josie's happy yelps reached him. A warm place had been fixed up for her in the corner of the kitchen. She lay on a blanket with her food and water bowls within each reach. Joey's heart lurched when she fell trying to stand up. He hurried over to her.

"No! No, Josie. Don't get up. Stay still," he said. When Josie lifted her head and ran her tongue over his cheek, Joey's eyes stung. "It's good to see you home, girl."

"She'll stay in the beauty shop while I'm at work and you're at school. The doctor says to keep her quiet." Mr. Johnson bent down and patted her head.

Later, dry and changed into warmer clothes, Joey edged downstairs and outside. He helped his mother close down the shop. Few trick-or-treaters braved the rainstorm.

Josie slept while they ate a pizza-and-salad dinner on paper plates. Then Mr. Johnson built a fire and Mama turned on the television. Joey watched from a distance, despite his mother's invitation to join them on the sofa.

When Mr. Johnson put up the kitchen gate and went upstairs with Mama, Joey went, too. He closed his bedroom door and finished his homework. He tossed Dog to the side of the bed as he crawled in. Just as he was falling asleep, he heard sounds coming from the kitchen. He jumped up and ran downstairs.

Josie was crying. Joey saw that she wanted to relieve herself. Although the dog was heavy, he managed to get her outside. Afterward they struggled back in. While he patted her dry, he was careful to avoid the raw patches and the broken leg. Josie's tail beat against the tile.

"You should hate me, Josie."

Her tail wagged harder. When he got up to leave, she hobbled to the gate. "Stay back, girl! Please!" But the dog whimpered.

"You win." With that, Joey left and came back. The warm, dark kitchen enfolded him as he spread out a plaid blanket and lay down next to Josie. Placing his robe over her, he nestled close enough to touch her. Before he had counted to twelve, he was asleep.

11

Joey rubbed at his face, feeling furry warmth. He turned on the hard floor to reach for his blanket. Nothing. In the wan morning light, Joey faced Josie. Her bright eyes startled him. The blanket was wadded around his feet. Quickly he checked the kitchen clock. 5:00 A.M. Good. He could make it to his bedroom before Mr. Johnson or Mama got up. "Tonight I'll bring my alarm clock, a pillow, and my sleeping bag," he whispered to Josie.

Josie's movements told him that she wanted to go out. Together they shuffled into the backyard. Joey flinched every time her right leg touched the ground. He wished he could carry her all the way. Back inside, he changed her water and gave her a treat. After a quick hug, he rushed upstairs, closing his door just before he heard the door at the far end of the hall open and shut.

Mr. Johnson spent Sunday working. He took off in the truck, calling to Joey to keep a careful eye on the Airedale terrier. Joey had pleaded exhaustion so that he could escape church. Toward lunchtime the doorbell rang. It was D.J. Together they entered the kitchen.

D.J. bent down and gently pushed Josie back into her prone position. Joey rummaged through the refrigerator. He piled bread, mustard, pickles, olives, hot dogs, and potato chips on the table, with cans of soda. Joey set the hot dogs to boil, putting in an extra one for Josie. He took out paper plates and arranged the condiments on them.

"She looks pretty good," D.J. remarked, placing his jacket

on the back of a chair. "Whoever hit her should go to jail. Will she walk with a limp?"

Joey swallowed. "No, the doctor said she won't."

"What a great dog! I mean, with two steel pins in her leg and getting banged up and bruised, she doesn't even snap or bite," said D.J., sitting on the floor next to Josie.

"I know."

D.J. stood up. "Come on, I'm hungry. You ready for the gifted test?"

Joey shrugged his shoulders. "Right now, getting into gifted isn't the big deal it was."

"Yes, it is. I know you belong in gifted. Shoot, half of the kids we know should be in it, but they don't speak up fast enough or act the way teachers like." D.J. stopped and nibbled on a potato chip.

Joey put the hot dogs onto a plate. He cut one into small pieces. When it cooled, he placed it in a plastic bowl. Josie practically inhaled the meat, licking the bowl while Joey held it. She licked his hand.

D.J. laughed. "She loves you."

Joey sighed. "She doesn't know what I did to her." He was silent for a moment. "About the gifted test, you didn't finish."

"I know you feel bad every time I go."

Joey started to protest, but D.J. silenced him. "No, it's the truth. I'd feel the same way if I were you. You should be going with me. All we do is work on projects, and most of them are easier than the science ones I've seen you set up and run."

A flush covered Joey's face. "I used to feel like that. Like if I was in gifted with you and Denise, then everyone would think I was smart. But now, I mean, even if I don't get into gifted, I'm still Joey Davis. Dumb enough to let Josie out, but smart enough to get her back."

Josie whimpered.

"What's wrong with her?" D.J. jumped up.

"Hey, girl, you want to go out? Or do you want some more hot dog?" Joey watched her tail move. "Okay." He helped her out and rewarded her with a little treat. "Drink some water. Wait a minute, it's time for your medicine." Quickly he cut off a piece of his hot dog, made a slit in the center, and stuck the capsule inside. Unknowingly, Josie gulped it down.

"The medicine makes her sleepy. She's fine now. Anyway, if I make gifted, I make it. If not, don't worry, D.J., we'll still be friends. You know that."

"Well, no matter what anybody says, if this gifted business was fair, you'd be in," insisted D.J. "If you're not gifted, then I'm not."

Just then Mr. Johnson strode in. "Winter's coming too soon. I've got to finish these jobs before the rains hit harder. Hi, D.J. Josie, stay!" he commanded.

"I fed her and gave her the medicine," said Joey. That made him think of something he had to do. "Oh, I have to give you this." He handed his stepfather the envelope from Doc. "For Josie's bills."

Mr. Johnson stared at him, then at the envelope. D.J. got up, cleared his place, ruffled Josie's ears, and left the kitchen.

Joey heard his friend go up to his bedroom and started to leave, too.

"Wait. Thanks for taking such good care of Josie. And, as for this, you keep it. Use it for your college fund," said Mr. Johnson.

"No. Like you said, sorry isn't enough. The money won't change what I did. I know that." Joey left before his stepfather could reply.

During the rest of the afternoon, the boys played in the bedroom. Even a telephone call from Chicago didn't ruin Joey's fun. Daddy was fine, happy, but tired and lonely. Over and over again he pressed Joey to spend Thanksgiving with him in Chicago. Joey hesitated, finally promising that he'd ask his mother. It was a relief to hang up and return to destroying monsters on the Nintendo screen.

Late that night, after everyone was asleep, Joey gathered his supplies and sneaked downstairs. Josie's nose was pressed against the wooden gate as if she'd been expecting him. Using the light of the moon, he made a cup of cocoa and grabbed a few cookies.

The sleeping bag and pillow softened the kitchen floor. Joey eased in, snuggling against Josie. When she whimpered during the night, he stroked her head, whispering consolations. Finally he took his pillow and laid it under the injured leg, careful to adjust the angle for comfort. Josie fell asleep, and Joey followed.

The soft beep-beep of the alarm clock sounded. Joey was in his own bed and sound asleep in minutes. When his mother came to wake him up, he felt as if he'd only had a few hours of solid sleep. Quickly, Mama hugged him. She was coughing and sneezing as she left his bedroom.

Joey had school and two hours of helping Doc at the drugstore ahead of him. He yawned.

Wednesday was the big test day. That morning Mr. Johnson drove Joey to school so that he could save all his energy for the test. While his stepfather concentrated on the road, Joey stared out the side window. Mr. Johnson remained a mystery. Although they hadn't had many private talks, the ones they'd had left a lot of questions. Joey didn't know how to ask the questions he wanted to. At last he just forged ahead. "Mr. Johnson, what happened to your parents?"

"My father took off somewhere and my mother gave me up to the special services when I was three months old."

"Didn't she want you?"

Mr. Johnson stopped for a red light. "She was sixteen when she had me. No skills. No support. She figured I'd have a better life adopted by a good family. Except that didn't happen."

"Uncle Mike?"

"A social worker who took a liking to me. I was good at basketball. Spent my life on the courts. Now, Uncle Mike was great, but a bad knee injury ended his pro career. He might have been a Doctor J. or Michael Jordan. Regardless, he was my hero."

"Do you know your mother?"

"She's dead. So is Uncle Mike. I never found my father." With that he slammed down on the clutch. The huge truck surged forward.

Joey held his breath. One more secret remained. He had to know.

"Mr. Johnson, when you were younger, what was the bad thing you did?"

"So I get to tell first. Okay. I stole a car and got caught. Uncle Mike was the social worker assigned to check on me," said Mr. Johnson. "He became my best friend. It took me a long time to trust him."

Joey slid a look at his stepfather. I can see why family and home mean so much to him, he thought. Him? I need to figure out what to call him.

They pulled up in front of the school. Before Joey got out of the truck, Mr. Johnson stopped him.

"No matter what happens today, your mother and I want you to do your best. That is all that matters to us, not whether you score high or not, but that you go in, take that test, and come out knowing that you tried your hardest." Mr. Johnson held out his hand.

Feeling more confident, Joey reached over and shook his stepfather's hand, startled at the pat on the shoulder he felt as he got out.

At nine o'clock, a resource teacher named Mr. Brooks came to get him. D.J. gave him a victory sign, Denise grinned, while Clark rolled his eyes. Buoyed, but tired, Joey left with Mr. Brooks. He took a seat in a small office at the end of the hall. For a while they just chatted. Joey relaxed. Mr. Brooks reminded him of his father.

For over two hours, with a few breaks, Joey completed the paper-and-pencil test. He responded to tasks that required him to compare and contrast numbers, figures, mathematical statements, to think about situations in logical and predictive ways, and to create solutions. His favorite tasks were the ones in which he had to draw and label different things that could be made from something else, like a square. This was the first interesting test he had ever taken. He worked hard. At last it ended.

Joey stretched while Mr. Brooks informed him that the

results should be ready in a week. Before he returned to his room, the teacher shared milk and doughnuts with him.

Back in the classroom, Joey took his seat, pleased that the test was over. At least I got a chance to try. Like Daddy, he thought. Going to the trouble to get tested is like Daddy fighting to get a chance to be interviewed.

"How did you do?" asked D.J.

Joey yawned. "I worked hard. But I won't know my scores for a week."

Almost in unison, his friends said, "Don't worry! You did fine!"

"Sometimes, especially at the end, my eyes felt like a tarsier's."

"No, please, not another one! I know a tarsier is a primate who looks a lot like a furry . . ." D.J. paused.

"Like a furry E.T.!" finished Denise.

"Right, Denise. It has big eyes, and I mean big. Each eye weighs more than its brain." Joey grinned. "The other strange thing about it doesn't really count."

"Tell us."

"Wait until my science report. But here's a clue: Think about a really scary movie our parents talk about sometimes. Think about a little girl and yucky green stuff." Joey waited.

Denise stared off. D.J. hit the desk, frustrated. Suddenly, Denise let out a laugh. "This time I got you, Joey Davis! I know the movie, *The Exorcist.* The tarsier can turn its head almost all the way around."

With a new sense of admiration, Joey nodded. Denise danced in her seat.

12

By Friday afternoon, Joey had put in his allotted hours at the drugstore and even more sleeping on the floor next to Josie. Tired, he arranged the first-aid shelves, stocking more flu medicines. With the strains of a piano playing above him, Joey finished emptying the last box.

"Hey, let's take a little break!" called Doc. "The rush won't start for about twenty minutes, and we haven't had a Feel Better soda in a long time."

From his stool, Joey examined the wall of memories behind Doc. A new photograph had been added. In it Doc was holding a little baby, dressed in pink. One of the photographs of Doc's wife had been shifted over to make room.

"Isn't that the most beautiful baby girl in the world? And she already talks! My youngest girl's daughter. Named her Elizabeth after my Elizabeth," commented Doc, reaching for the soda glasses. "New life that is part of me and my beloved Elizabeth."

"You moved some of the pictures around," Joey said.

Doc nodded. "You've been doing some moving around, too, I think. I notice you've been coming in here and working hard, yawning three hundred times an hour and not talking about anything except Josie. Not even that gifted test. But I bet you still haven't gotten that name problem for your stepfather worked out yet, have you? It's still 'Mr. Johnson,' right?"

Joey stared at Doc. He didn't miss a thing!

"Here, is this soda big enough for you?"

"Plenty big. Thanks, Doc. It's strange. I don't feel like

everything depends on whether or not I passed that test."

"Good. Here's your pay for the week. What are you going to do with the money?" asked Doc.

"Keep paying for Josie's vet bills."

"That's what I wanted to hear. I'm going to open up the pharmacy in January. By then I'll have somebody full time. But I'll still need you when you have some time."

"Sure, Doc; you can count on me."

Fridays were hard for everyone. By the time Joey got home, helped his mother, and took care of Josie, he was too exhausted for dinner. Mr. Johnson was working the late shift. His mother was soaking in a long, hot bath. Joey turned on the telephone answering machine. He'd call his father tomorrow.

In the mail his father had sent him a Chicago Bears sweatshirt. Joey pulled it on. A fire burned in the fireplace. Josie whimpered steadily when Joey closed the gate to go upstairs to bed. He relented and helped her into the living room, where they fell asleep in a heap on the floor.

Saturday morning sunshine poured in. Joey stirred. At the bottom of his bed, Josie turned in her sleep. Feeling the motion, Joey sat up. How did he end up in here? And with Josie.

His door was closed. The clock said 7:00 A.M. Quietly he got up and went to the door. From the bathroom he heard his mother and stepfather in the kitchen. Josie whimpered. Joey dropped his toothbrush and ran into his bedroom to help Josie downstairs so that she could go outside.

Back inside he gave her a treat. Then he got dressed. He was due at Doc's in the afternoon. Maybe business would be slow.

"Joey, do you have a couple of hours this morning? I could use your help on a small paint job I have to complete. Your mother can watch Josie in the beauty shop," said Mr. Johnson, wiping his mouth.

"Franklin, that sounds like a lot for one day. Joey's working for Doc this afternoon," Mama said.

This time Joey was the one who made up his mind. He thought quickly. I can do both. If I don't go, he may never ask me again.

"I'll eat and get dressed and then I'll be ready to go," replied Joey, digging into the stack of pancakes.

While other vehicles inched along, the 1953 Chevy pickup truck roared toward its destination.

"How did Josie end up in bed with me?" asked Joey. "How did I end up in bed?"

Mr. Johnson smiled. "Well, since the two of you have been spending your nights together, I figured you might as well be comfortable."

"You saw us in the kitchen? You never said anything."

Mr. Johnson shrugged his shoulders, "I must admit I was jealous at first. But you two—well, Josie loving you is good."

They turned up a road that seemed familiar. Joey watched the trees bend and twist in the wind. They were going to see Mr. and Mrs. Hodges, that nice couple for whom they'd put in the greenhouse window.

In the hours of work that they shared, Joey learned to remove ventilator panels and tape windows. In less time than they had allowed, the bathroom was painted and everything cleaned up and stored in the truck. Mr. Johnson accepted the check from Mr. Hodges. Then he dropped Joey off at the drugstore on the way to his next job.

"Good work, Joey," Mr. Johnson said before he drove off. "I'm glad you're back in the Front Seat Club."

Joey smiled.

All afternoon, he worked at Doc's. Once home, he checked on Josie and helped close down the beauty shop. His mother headed straight to bed. When he heard the familiar sounds of the '53 Chevy pickup truck, he grabbed his jacket and hurried out the back door.

"Hey, Joey. Come on into the garage with me," his stepfather called out as he shut the truck door. "We need to straighten it up and then unload."

The garage needed some cleaning. Mr. Johnson had become too busy with jobs to keep it orderly. As usual, they fell into a silent rhythm as they worked. When they had finished, Mr. Johnson sat down on the workbench. Paint, oil, veneer, and wood smells mingled in the garage.

"Mama's in bed," Joey reported.

"I know. I called her earlier. She's catching a cold. Hope it's not the flu. Here." Mr. Johnson handed Joey a sandwich and a drink from the cooler. Together they ate.

"You know that talk we had about the friend of mine who got into trouble?" Joey asked

"Yes."

"Well, he straightened it out."

"Face to face, I hope," replied Mr. Johnson.

"Yes, even though my friend was scared," Joey said.

"Tell your friend I'm proud of him."

Joey grinned.

That night Joey's father called. "Son, I managed to get airline tickets! I'll be in Berkeley for Thanksgiving. Isn't that great?" his father asked.

"Great, Daddy. I'll talk to Mama." Joey's stomach started to hurt.

"Everything will work out fine, Son. I've missed you so. I can't wait to see you."

Back in his bedroom, Joey sought the photograph of his family. Having to decide who to spend Thanksgiving with was hard.

I have two parents. They love me. So does Josie. Mr. Johnson and I are talking. But it feels so confusing, and I'm stuck in the middle. I've got to do something.

Joey got up. He wrote a letter to his father. When his mother got up on Sunday morning, he caught her alone. His stepfather was working on the truck.

"Mama, I have to tell you something about Thanksgiving. Daddy's flying here. I made up my own mind: I'm going to eat two dinners. One with Daddy and one with you and Mr. Johnson and Josie," Joey announced. "That's what I wrote to Daddy. I want it official."

His mother tugged at the belt of her terry-cloth robe. Her hair was uncombed, and she looked ill. "Honey, are you sure? We can try to work something out and have your father here."

"No, Mama. I'd be too nervous. This is the way I want it. Please?" he asked.

Mama grinned. "When in the world did my little boy start turning into a man? Making up his mind about things like this? Working jobs? I better keep my eye on you, honey. I don't want to lose you to that nutty world out there too soon." She hugged him.

"You won't, Mama. I promise," Joey murmured.

On Wednesday, Mrs. Hamlin called Joey to her desk. There was a new science bulletin board to put up. He was thinking about putting together one about dolphins, porpoises, and whales. They were such a magnificent group. Questions about animal intelligence and their ability to communicate could be shared and discussed. His head hummed with ideas.

"Joey, Mrs. Mack wants to see you in her office," she said.

It was only a week since he'd sat in the room with Mr. Brooks. On the way to the office he saw Miss Alder bringing her class from the library and he waved.

She beckoned to him. "I know you got tested for gifted, and my fingers are crossed. What do you wish?" she asked, smiling.

That was a hard one, but then Joey knew. "I wish I was a lucky newborn loggerhead sea turtle, Miss Alder." He waited to see if she understood. Her warm laugh told him she did.

"Joey Davis, I miss you so much. Good luck."

The idea of forcing his way out of one of the hundreds of soft white eggs hatched by a mother loggerhead and then inching across the beach toward the sea, hoping that he was headed the right way, frightened him. One false flip, belly up, and the tiny turtle was a goner. One turn in the wrong direction, and the chance for the safety of the sea disappeared. And there was always the danger of baby loggerheads getting plucked up by the hordes of waiting seabirds. Joey shivered. Being a lucky loggerhead wasn't easy.

When Mrs. Mack ushered him into her office, Joey felt a sudden rush. Mr. Brooks sat there. On the other side of the resource teacher sat his mother and Mr. Johnson!

"Honey, I called your father, and he'll talk with you tonight. Come sit here, next to us," she said. She was dressed as if she were going to church.

Mr. Johnson just nodded. But Joey felt buttressed between the two of them. He wondered if the truck was outside. Probably.

The principal took her seat behind the wooden desk with papers neatly stacked in separate piles. She gestured to Mr. Brooks. Mr. Brooks took a breath and focused his attention on the adults. "Joey took a test that assesses various kinds of intelligence. It can detect divergent thinking, perceiving the world in creative ways, the ability to use logic, space, and symbols in unusual situations, and more."

"How did Joey do?" pressed Mama.

"Well, Mrs. Johnson, the test can give us an idea of where a young person's unique gifts may be. Joey's talent is in science."

Mrs. Mack nodded, reached for the folder and scanned the conclusions. "Joey, you have quite advanced thinking skills. You can see unexpected relationships and explain them."

"This is wonderful. Franklin, did you hear that?" Mama beamed.

Mr. Johnson smiled. "I sure did."

The principal continued. "With Miss Alder's help, Mr. Brooks and I have done some research. The University of

California at Berkeley's Lawrence Hall of Science offers a program for gifted young scientists. They want you, Joey," said Mrs. Mack. "That means attending classes on some Saturdays each month and on weekdays during the summer. They need an answer right away."

"Wonderful!" exclaimed Mr. Johnson. "I know you can do it."

"But would I still get to go to gifted class here with D.J. and Denise?" asked Joey.

Mrs. Mack spoke. "You'll have to make a choice between the two programs. With more budget cuts coming, we are not increasing our gifted program here at school, but there is room for one more student."

Joey reviewed the responsibilities he had taken on: working at Doc's to pay off Josie's vet bills; working with Mr. Johnson; and keeping up with his regular schoolwork. He knew that Doc, Mama, and Mr. Johnson would help him. But can I do it all? he wondered. Plus I have to deal with Daddy flying in and out. Joey's mind tumbled over and over. At the same time, his heart soared at the thought of studying at a fancy place like the Lawrence Hall of Science! Imagine me, Joey Davis, being in a gifted class there. Wow!

Mr. Johnson asked, "When does Joey have to decide?"

Mrs. Mack sighed. "I'm sorry, but we need to know by Monday. You can speak with the teachers in both programs if you want to."

Joey thought fast. If I choose the gifted program here at school, I get to walk out with D.J. and Denise and show Mrs. Hamlin, Clark, and his bunch how smart I really am. But what else would I get? Is being able to show them up more important than doing what I love?

"Joey, please listen. This is very serious. You only have a few days to decide. You can talk it over with your father. Franklin and I will support any decision you make. Are you paying attention me?" Mama reached over and shook him a little.

Joey looked straight at the adults surrounding him. "Mama, I made my choice. I love natural science! I want to be in the program at the Lawrence Hall of Science."

Everyone grinned, relieved and happy. After handshakes all the way around, Joey waved good-bye to Mama and Mr. Johnson. Miss Alder was just going into her room.

"You knew! All this time, you knew," he said.

Miss Alder stopped and put her hands on her hips. "Well, you were my best science-center leader. Did you go with your heart and mind?"

Joey nodded. "Lawrence Hall of Science, here I come."

He shared the news with D.J. and Denise. Mrs. Hamlin and Clark acted as if nothing had happened. But Joey knew better.

"I'm going to have to make you a card, Joey," Denise announced. "A very gifted one."

When the school day ended, Joey and D.J. got their bikes.

"I want to hear everything that happened. I'll go with you to Doc's. I can't stay long. Mama wants me home. But I want to treat you to a Feel Better soda." The boys took off.

Doc made the sodas, congratulated Joey, and then hurried to talk with a salesman about supplies for the pharmacy. Joey leaned back on the stool. The music swung, up-tempo songs.

After D.J. left, Joey worked in aisle two, where some kids had overturned a carton of bubble-gum balls. Only three customers were in the store. Joey hummed as he worked.

"Your time is up," Doc called. "Let's sit at the soda fountain."

Doc listened intently as Joey explained the unexpected events of the day. Whenever he skipped something, Doc made him go back. As Joey heard himself talk, the decision to go to the Lawrence Hall of Science felt just right.

"You know what my best friend said to me once when she was very ill? 'Darling, it's worth it to stay alive, just for the surprises.' And she didn't mean good or bad surprises—she just meant surprises. Oh, I miss her. So, my friend, you've experienced a day packed with surprises. Remember when I told you that you were the most fortunate of young men? Now you are learning how to act like one." Doc hugged Joey.

Dinner conversation centered around the meeting at school. Joey called his father and told him the good news. Later that evening, when Mr. Johnson locked Josie inside the kitchen, Joey hurriedly completed his homework. Sleeping on the hard kitchen floor wasn't easy, but he was committed to staying with Josie until she was fully recovered.

He gathered up his bedding, waiting for the bedroom door at the end of the hall to close. It finally did. Joey sneaked down the stairs. But the kitchen wasn't empty. Mr. Johnson was there.

"How long can you go on like this?" he asked.

Joey stood there.

"I mean, you yawn and stumble around with bags under your eyes. Enough is enough." Mr. Johnson got up from the kitchen table. "Josie is fine in here. Warm. Fed. Happy. Go on up to bed."

"I can't. I know she's your dog, but I can't leave her alone at night, not with her leg still hurt," Joey said, clutching the sleeping bag closer.

Josie wagged her tail.

"Seems like she's your dog, too, Joey. What are we going to do?"

Joey took a long look at his stepfather. He seemed different. Less a stranger. Certainly not a Mr. Johnson.

"Seems like you're taking on too much," said Mr. Johnson. "I think that we should put going out on the truck on hold."

Joey stared at his bare feet. "Can I try to do it all for a while and see how it works out? I want to go out on the truck with you and Josie. And I want to get to level three. What *is* level three?" he asked, realizing that he didn't even know.

"Cutter," Mr. Johnson replied. "You learn how to use the level, tape measures, the chalk line, as well as combination and framing squares for precise measurement. And you learn how to cut. Those cutting tools can be dangerous if you don't know what you're doing and aren't patient. When you get to level three, I'll buy you your own saw, a simple one to start with."

"I'll make it there," Joey said.

"Frankly, I'd be surprised if you didn't. If you're this stubborn about going out, then we'll try it a few times and see." With that, Mr. Johnson got up and left.

A few minutes later he returned. "This is an air mattress. Since you are so bound and determined to sleep with Miss Josie, the prima donna, your mother and I want you to be comfortable and get some good, deep sleep. Now, when Josie gets stronger, both of you go upstairs to bed."

"Mama knew about this?" Joey sank down onto the air mattress. Josie nestled next to him.

"Your mother knows everything that goes on." Mr. Johnson chuckled. "Now go to sleep. This has been some day."

The next two days flowed into each other. Joey handled the science center and concentrated on work. He, D.J., and Denise stayed in their own cluster. Joey glanced at Clark, who was still at the desk by Mrs. Hamlin. He looked sloppy, angry, and miserable. Clark has a problem with himself and he's not moving anywhere with it but down. I'm just going to keep my distance, Joey decided. He knew that Denise and D.J. felt the same way.

After school he biked to his job at Doc's. With the air mattress and sound sleep, Joey felt stronger. He'd mailed the letter to his father about having two Thanksgiving dinners. Having that resolved helped.

On Friday evening, Mama was exhausted from the cold she'd had all week and went straight from work to bed. Joey talked to his father. It looked as if they'd go out for Thanksgiving dinner or eat with some of his father's relatives. Joey hung up as the kitchen door opened and Mr. Johnson came in.

"I bet your mother is knocked out. Right?" asked Mr. Johnson, petting Josie.

"She sure is. I made her some tea."

"Let me check on her. Then we'll get something to eat and celebrate your victory." He hurried up the stairs.

When he returned, he shook his head. "She's beat. Let's go get her some wonton soup," he said.

Mr. Johnson had backed the truck into the backyard. Joey thought how unusual that was. Under the outside lights,

Joey saw bold, shiny, bright-red letters on the driver's side of the pickup truck. Curious, he walked closer and read the words under his breath: JOHNSON & FAMILY, CONTRACTORS.

Joey stood there, rooted to the spot, barely hearing Josie bark. Johnson and Family, Contractors, he repeated to himself. Mama and Daddy will always be my real family. No matter where Daddy lives.

An unexpected ache gripped him. The divorce still hurt. Daddy and Mama are really divorced. They won't get married to each other again. The admission shook Joey.

He knew that Mr. Johnson was standing behind him, waiting for him to say something about the words on the side of the truck. "I like red," Joey said. "It looks real professional." Mr. Johnson moved around him and opened the door to the cab. "That's nice of you to say."

Joey helped Josie up onto the front seat between him and Mr. Johnson. The quiet inside the truck wasn't tense. It was just a kind of tired quiet.

On the way back from the Chinese restaurant, Joey was still thoughtful. *Johnson & Family, Contractors* was what the sign said. But what family did it refer to? Mama. Josie. Of course Mr. Johnson. What about me?

"You're looking pretty gloomy over there. Anything wrong? Did something happen at school?"

"No, nothing's wrong, just mixed up," Joey answered.

"Join the club!"

"You get mixed up?" Joey was shocked. Mr. Johnson sure fit the description of Doc's solid man.

Mr. Johnson drove silently for a few blocks. "Sometimes I feel confused about what to do, even about what is the right thing to say, especially with you, your mother, and your father. I get frustrated and uncertain about trying to make it as a contractor and fighting the odds. But I keep on working and taking care of my family. Eventually, things straighten out."

Work, repeated Joey in his head. Mr. Johnson is right. Working with the science, at Doc's, and out on the truck helped make his life clearer.

As the houses and streets sped past, Josie nestled closer. Joey scratched her behind her ears.

"Joey, hey, can you wipe the front window for me. It's all fogged up. The towel should be near you. I've got my hands full with this traffic," said Mr. Johnson.

"Okay, Mr. J." The words sprang out of his mouth before Joey knew it. The name fit his stepfather—*Mr. J.* He wondered how Mr. Johnson felt about it. Joey wiped down the window. He replaced the towel. Josie leaned against him.

Nervously, Joey watched automobiles scampering about from lane to lane in disorder. The truck moved from one section of the freeway to the next, settling into a steady pattern that would take them to the off ramp not far from the house.

"I like that name, Joey," said his stepfather, accelerating a bit. "It took me a lot longer to come up with *Uncle Mike.* Now I can understand how he felt when I did."

"How, Mr. J.?"

"Like he belonged. Like he was a real part of my life and I was a real part of his. Thanks, Joey."

Joey couldn't speak, so he nodded. Josie licked his face.

In no time at all, they were home. Joey clutched bags of

food while his stepfather helped Josie out. The three of them headed for the house. Mr. Johnson took some of the bags and hurried on.

Joey stopped and gazed up at the muddy sky. He knew that above the clouds airplanes flew and stars shone. And he was learning that below the clouds life moved on, just like Doc said. Bad things happened. But no matter what, I'll never be a shadow man, Joey swore to himself.

Josie yelped at him, her tail wagging. Joey looked down at her, smelled the food, and felt the warmth coming from the kitchen.

Joey climbed the steps and walked through the kitchen door, his head high.